Claire:
the Lost Fae

Aithne Jarretta

Published in U.S.A. by Aithne Jarretta
COPYRIGHT 2012

http://aithnejarretta.com

Cover and book design
P.S. Strickland

ISBN: 0615604668
ISBN-13: 978-0615604664
Bird of Paradise Publishing
Clearwater, FL

This Novella is

dedicated to

Amanda

Bless You

CONTENTS

1 Threshold: Angels Speak   8

2 Fae Dreaming   31

3 Insights of the Heart   44

4 Witch in a Bubble   81

5 Elemental Gateway   85

6 Wicked   87

7 Elemental   97

8 Illusions   106

9 Screaming Mojo   121

10 Fascination   132

11 Magical Menagerie   146

12 *Òran Mór*   159

Epilogue   168

Welcome to the Thinning Veil

Six hundred years ago, earth time, the great Oracle of Annwn, Kingdom of the Fae foretold the coming of a great darkness. It is said this wickedness would gain its foothold within the Earthly realm and spread through the magical veil into Annwn. To halt the spread of evil, the three great ruling Houses of Worthy in the realm of Annwn must unite.

Claire is a potent connection and has been lost through life circumstances. But just because one wanders doesn't mean their journey lacks meaning. When found, will Claire agree to the necessary union?

| Part One |
Dreams Unwind
*While we are sleeping angels have
conversations with our souls.
Unknown*

* * * * * * * * *

[1] Threshold: Angels Speak

Tender green leaves brushed against Claire's arm as she slipped between an oak tree and a neatly trimmed park bush. She pushed the leaves aside, sat against the rough tree bark, and wrapped her blanket over bare arms.

Exhaustion weighed her spirit down with nighttime dread.

Ocean breezes coming from San Francisco bay combined with her travel weariness and gave a sense of bone deep cold.

She shivered, curled knees up to her chest and rested furrowed forehead on the ragged denim of her jeans.

Exhaustion equaled danger in her magical world. The need for rest could weaken and dull senses that should be sharp and alert.

Just close my eyes...a few minutes...

A rumbling in her stomach made Claire gnaw her lower lip. She would find food later. The alleys and streets of San Francisco had been her new home for three days. "Relax," she whispered to her weary body. "Food in the morning... Sleep a bit first."

As though a holographic world surrounded Claire, fragmented edges of a horrific dream pummeled her into an emotional abyss.

Blackness misted the edges of this outland dream realm, rippled eerily upon the airwaves and moved outward into the summer night.

Claire groaned.

In her nightmare, the surface of a braided rug skinned sensitive palms and youthful knees. Tiny fingers searched across the floor for a hiding place. In her heart, she longed to discover hope. Its essence proved completely elusive.

An atmosphere of anger and fear blazed around her.

That was how she saw the world. She was tiny. Everything else was big and fearsome. Terror filled her life even at seven years old.

Smack!

Claire screamed and crawled across the floor fast, but could not get away from Ms. Bierce's anger. Third foster mother in as many months, Ms. Bierce was the biggest and instantly the meanest.

Snotty nose interfered with breathing and tear filled eyes blurred everything, but did not hide the horror. Claire sniffled and tried to stand up as a last resort to get off the rough surface of the rug. She rubbed the back of a shaky hand across her face.

The massive woman shoved. The corner of a table jammed into Claire's back. Oxygen exploded from her lungs and carried a scream of desperation.

Smack!

The air across the room parted magically on startling electrical waves. Within a heavenly light a beautiful woman shouted, "Stop that!"

Claire shoved curls away from her face, wiped eyes and stared. The glow around the woman made

Claire think she was an angel.

"I know you did it!" screeched Ms. Bierce.

It was as though she did not see the woman who had appeared.

"No! No, I didn't! Joey broke it," Claire wailed.

"Back to the convent!" Ms. Bierce's heavy bosom jostled as she shook a fist at Claire. "Wicked devil's spawn!" She moved as though to kick Claire.

The angel stepped closer. "I'm warning you!"

Ms. Bierce advanced.

The angel's arm swept forward with great magical force.

Ms. Bierce flew backward across the room and crashed into the china cabinet. Dishes and crystal shattered. Ms. Bierce's cussing filled the room with a loathing aura.

The angel faded away.

"Come back," Claire pleaded. But it was no use.

Claire woke. Heart wrenching sobs shook her whole body. She wiped sorrow filled tears from hot cheeks. That same nightmare had haunted her for twelve years. Nothing ever changed.

The angel always left.

Lights outlining the magnificent Golden Gate Bridge blurred through her tears. The blanket had slipped down so she pulled the frayed edges up tighter around her shoulders and scrunched back against the tree trunk, which helped shelter her within a bushy shrine.

An aura of summer scents; green grass, bark and plush leaves hid her from the outside world.

San Francisco was just another stop on her journey fleeing constant danger.

Her odyssey for a safe haven was no different

than looking for a pot of gold at the end of a rainbow. Completely elusive.

Voices in the park this late at night traveled upon the air.

Claire knew the people behind those voices were searching for her. She didn't understand the specifics why, but it wasn't the first time she had been chased.

When someone pursued her, it usually had something to do with her magic. Sometimes people just wanted her to leave or someone was actually trying to kill her.

"Know she's here somewhere," a harsh voice growled.

"That's what you said about the docks." This man's voice had a belligerent quality.

Annoying bastard. She bit back a retort because there was no sense in letting them know her location.

Apparently his companion thought the same thing. "Shut yer face. All you do is whine and complain."

She had gotten away from these stalkers at the docks. The big question was, how'd they find her again?

Claire could see them now through her protective shield of branches and leaves.

It was the shorter fat man that made her flinch. He was the one with a harsh voice. The combination of a square nose, droopy jowl and large ears made him one of the ugliest men she had ever seen.

His next words revealed the true reason for her anxiety.

"I can smell her," short jowly fatso said, "when she uses her magic."

The tall skinny man snorted. "I smell ocean, grass and fish. Not witch."

She didn't dare move or breathe. That answered the question how that nasty mutt face kept finding her. *That's it. No more magic.*

"Don't move—even blink," said a clear masculine voice within her head.

Claire froze. Hearing voices in her head was nothing new. In the magical world everything in the universe spoke through vibration.

She always understood that connection and frequently listened to the wisdom that came from a greater universal power.

"Who are you?" Even in her own head the words cracked with tension. *"Friend or foe?"*

"Friend. They know you're close."

The marauders stood within feet of her bushy refuge.

She had a perfect view of the tall man's knees.

Within her mind, she sent finely tuned sensors toward the man communicating in mind speak. She needed to read his magical signature better.

Quiet moments passed while the two stalkers searched the park clearing.

Leaves on the closest shrub moved and whispered upon an invisible breeze. That was the sign she had been waiting for. The leaves carried an understandable reading from the man that had spoken within her mind.

He wasn't lying. He was there to help.

"What are you going to do?" she asked while watching short fatso sniff the air.

"Get you away. No matter what happens, stay where you are."

She answered in her head. *"Okay."*

Eyes wide open, afraid to blink, she saw

fragmented bursts of conflict.

The tall man yelled. The sound mingled with growls and curses.

Bridge lights backlit three silhouettes fighting with strange looking weapons.

Something, Claire thought it was a magical ray of power, hit the dog face man. He was flung through the air, but managed to stop his trajectory.

The dog face man levitated in midair and laughed with maniacal glee.

One silhouette wore a long coat. She realized that was her rescuer. The long coat swung out cape like every time the man moved. A mask, fashioned to look like a mythical animal head hid his identity.

The two marauders flanked the newcomer and attacked.

Claire leaned forward and dared to brush a branch downward. That freed up her view and she saw fast movement in close proximity. The three combatants were so close together she could not distinguish the good guy from the wicked stalkers.

A deathly scream split the night airwaves.

The sound of death sent horror bumps along her arms. An accompanying thump as the body landed close to her hideaway enforced a deep seated dread.

She had a clear view of wide, black eyes staring in death.

It was the tall thin man. His whiny voice silenced forever.

Miniature black shapes with pointed wings and screeching voices swooped in. As though they were devouring him, he began to vanish limb by limb.

A daemon, Claire thought with a shudder. She had seen those black hellion cleaners before. Evil always cleared up so the average folk didn't know the truth about their existence.

She had seen enough. Legs tucked up against her chest, she lowered eyes and pressed them against the denim covering her knees.

The night sounds of ocean, distant traffic, more cussing and the clash of steel pounded in her ears. Not seeing the horror failed to protect her because she experienced every movement through the sensation of feeling as though the conflict actually touched her skin.

She growled in frustration and raised her head. Night clouds that had hidden the full moon coursed across the sky on a western wind. Lunar silver spread earthward in a magical blessing.

An eerie silence descended in the park as though the silvering moonbeams washed every molecule of wickedness away.

"Come out, Claire."

Sudden caution shot through Claire and made the hair on her neck fizzle. The sensation compelled her to stay where she was even with the knowledge that her rescuer knew her exact location.

"You know my name? How?"

"Yes," he answered. *"I'll explain later. For now we must move fast. Grismere got away. He'll be back with reinforcements."*

"He smells magic."

"Because they're hounds. That's why we must go."

Claire crawled out of the bush. "Eugh! What's that smell?"

The man grabbed her, clamped a hand over her mouth, and then everything she could see melted into a maddening vortex of hot air.

The wind spun around them, whipped her

cheeks and grabbed the old blanket. She clutched the threadbare coverlet because it was her only source of warmth.

Whoosh!

"Let it go!" the man yelled in her ear.

She shook her head. The blanket twisted from her grasp and flew away. She watched the blanket's harried flight into the dark night sky.

The sudden absence left an empty hole in her chest.

Sister Teresa Blandina had given her that blanket for her fifteenth birthday. The blue softness and comfort was the only true birthday gift she ever remembered receiving.

Now, the blanket was gone.

They landed on a hillside dotted with old headstones. She shoved away from her rescuer. "Who are you? Didn't you hear me? That creep can smell magic! He'll follow us!"

"No. He can't follow. Besides, that old blanket will confuse the scent."

"Dammit! That *old blanket* and the clothes on my body are all I own. I'm asking *again*, who are you?"

"Name's Leeson. We'll get you a new blanket."

She growled. "Well Leeson," she said, fisting her fingers. "We need to get out of here."

"We're safe for now."

Exasperation spread from her belly upward. The resulting heat made her head feel on the verge of explosion. "Are you a brainless idiot?"

He peeled the mask off, revealing high cheekbones and mussed dark hair with cinnamon highlights shining from the moon glow. With a twist, he shoved the mask into a pocket of the long coat. "The hound can't track us here."

She hissed through her teeth. "That's just peachy! I don't believe you. You can stay. I'm going!"

He grabbed her arm. "No."

"Let me go, you bastard!" Claire wiggled and pulled. She could magic herself free but that would have called Grismere the hound to them.

"Be still," Leeson said, and shook her.

A large breath burst from her lungs and she went limp.

"Stop screeching. You have to stay close," he said as his eyes narrowed. "Figure it out. My coat hides us."

Energy buzzed through his hands where he held her upper arms.

At first she couldn't breathe, but then shallow breaths eased heightened senses. The sensation of his magic transference slowed her heart beat. A chill spread into her fingers. She rubbed them together trying to return warmth.

"There now," he said, making his voice softer. Moon glow shifted his expression between shadow and light. "Feel better?"

"What did you do to me?"

"Slowed your metabolism," he answered. "You may not realize, but your stress affects your magic. That mongrel and his pack can follow your magical scent. So it's imperative you stay calm and close."

"Fine. Just be sure you know, I don't agree," she insisted and lifted her chin to emphasize her point. "Why are we in a cemetery?"

"Looking for the Tower of Winds." He pulled a coat sleeve away from his hand. The object worn there definitely wasn't a watch. He twisted a knob and cocked his head to better read the face.

"Compass says we need to go this way." He

grabbed her hand and started walking fast without more comment.

"Your stride is twice mine! Slow down!"

He didn't slow down or release her hand. "You're screeching again."

Claire stumbled on an old tombstone that had fallen over. "Ow!"

His coat hides us from the hounds? Well try feeling this then. She sent him a jolt of electrical magic through her palm.

He gripped her hand harder. Through clenched teeth, he hissed, "Don't do that."

"Let. Me. Go."

"No. The tower is just over there."

Furious didn't begin to describe the plethora of emotions raging just under her skin. "I don't see a tower," she snapped while jerking her hand back.

Despite her efforts, they remained attached in a tug of war fueled by stubbornness.

"Fancy name for a mausoleum," he said, completely undaunted by her foul mood. "Eight sides. Each one depicting a carving of a wind god. All based on the Greek wind deities. That's where we'll get our instructions."

"You're just trying to distract me."

He paused to look at the area around them.

Claire pulled ahead. "Next, you're going to tell me some make believe Greek wind god will show us which way to go."

"In a manner of speaking." He indicated a glistening white marble mausoleum with a star studded pointed cap. Each star glistened in the night sky. The lighting effect formed a halo that illuminated the windblown weathervane attached to the top of the Greek inspired building.

Claire grunted. The copper figure depicted a

young woman clasping a long scarf or blanket. The wind battered them. "Funny."

"Perhaps not, but the symbolism fits perfectly." He flicked his wrist and changed the directional arrow to south. "Let's go," he said, and guided her toward the path the weathervane had originally pointed.

"If the hounds can follow our scent, then what good does it do to point them south?"

Leeson laughed. "Because the wind deity will carry our scent that way. We do have magical helpers." Moonlight shadowed his eyes and he frowned at her. "You realize that, don't you?"

"Humph," she said, and rolled her eyes. "Wind never cooperated for me."

"Then you must work on your connection to the web of power."

"Yeah right." She tried once more to pull her hand away from his without success. "Is there a college course for that? Wind Power 101?"

"This is no time to be sarcastic," he replied, and then pulled her hand.

Attached as they were, she collided with solid muscular chest.

"Think like this," he said close to her face. "The conflict in the park is point A. This cemetery and that weathervane is B. Our next destination will be point C. As long as we hang around *between* points, we leave a magical marker. Or in this case, scent. Understand?"

She ground her teeth and pursed lips while giving him her harshest glare.

"You're stalling. Do you understand?" he asked, and squeezed her hand to elicit a response.

"Grrr...Yes!"

"Good," he remarked, and nodded to the area

behind her. "We're here."

Claire stepped back and turned. An old wrought iron fence enclosed this section of the cemetery. The gate leading to the secluded corner stood ajar. She pushed and the piercing sound of rusted metal moving scratched along her spine.

Inside, they walked to the center and glanced around. The only sound around them came from tree leaves whispering in the night breeze.

"This way," Leeson said. He released her hand and rested his on the small of her back.

Claire moved forward until she arrived in front of a stone angel.

The angel was beautiful and stood at least six feet tall perched upon a solid marble base. The square base was embellished with intricate grapevines lush with ripened fruit.

With a horn in one hand and the other extended as though to help the weary *(or dead?)*, the angel protected the northeast corner of a secluded memorial garden.

Claire didn't understand how she knew this information, she just did.

"The highest arc in the wing," Leeson whispered in a tone of reverence. "That's the key to our next step."

They brushed aside the draping foliage of a weeping willow.

Claire stared up at the angel. Memory flashed in a familiar face, but the image seen in a long ago recollection vanished quickly from her mind.

She felt a tug in her hair. "Ouch! Rude! Why'd you do that?"

He held up one of her long black hairs so she could see his next move. With a gentle motion, Leeson brushed her hair up, and into the highest feather of the angel's wing.

Air and divine magic breathed upon them. The wing spread wide. Feathers ruffled, and then wrapped them in close softness.

Warmth and sheltering love cocooned them.

Claire's natural reaction was to lean into the wondrous sensation and surrender to the heavenly presence.

With unexpected abruptness, the earth fell away.

She could not stop the scream that burst from her lungs.

They landed in a pitch black hole.

The sudden change from loving embrace to hellish abyss birthed a pit of betrayal in her belly. "I will never trust another angel as long as I live."

The intensity of her anger gave them a faint magical glow—just enough to see. She knew the light was her magic reacting to fury.

"That's a strong statement," Leeson said while he sent a finger to touch the edge of light surrounding her. The magical illumination pinged him with an electrical shock.

He quirked a brow, and asked, "What did angels ever do to you?"

"Nothing good," Claire growled. She didn't want to tell him about her abandonment issues. Parents dying tragically when she was barely five; then convent life with a revolving in/out door, and her reoccurring nightmare where the angel vanished every single time.

In an obvious ploy to change the subject, he remarked, "This place smells like hell." He made a weird motion with his hand. A wand appeared between his fingers and magic lights flew from the tip. Everything within several feet around them glowed in a surreal blue intensity.

"Phew!" he said while his arm came up to cover his nose. "Wraythe." He swung the wand in his other hand and red magic burst outward. The spell hit a black shape on the earthen wall.

It screamed and advanced, bringing the odor closer.

Leeson hit the creature again with another blast.

"Stop it!" Claire stepped in front of him and knocked his wand down. "Don't attack."

She faced the wraythe. "I'm sorry. He doesn't realize I am your friend," she said formally, hoping to appease the wraythe's anger.

The creature paused and studied her through depthless eyes.

"Your kin saved me at the docks. I'm Claire."

The wraythe nodded and motioned for them to proceed down the underground passageway.

"I was right," Claire hissed. "You are an idiot. They will hide our scent. That's how I got away from Grismere at the docks."

"Wraythe are putrid."

"Obviously we disagree. I've known you for what? Thirty minutes and find you very annoying."

"You don't *know* me," Leeson said.

"Well as far as rescuers go you are infuriating and a pain in the ass."

"Humph," he said, and held the wand high enough to light the path. "Sure your nuns would approve of such language?"

"I'm finished with the nuns."

"Yet you were always protected at the convent. Didn't you learn about gratitude while there?"

Claire stopped. The passage split into three directions. She closed her eyes and tried to feel the route they should take. "Gratitude has many veins."

"Really? You don't say." He waved to their right side. "Like the paths in front of us?"

A subtle breath of air passed over her cheeks. "This way," she said, and turned left. At this point she wanted to be in control so she spoke even though she had no idea where they were going.

"How did you decide that?"

"Because," she answered, and marched forward with determination. "There's fresh air coming from this tunnel."

"Fresh air could mean anything."

"But it doesn't." She noticed that he avoided contact with her glow even though the magical energy had calmed down and was much fainter. "How did you find me in the park? And where are you from?"

"Humm?"

"You heard me," Claire said while pausing on the path.

Leeson collided with her backside. "Yes. I did. If you must know, I was tracking the hounds. This is my city and I don't like packs of creatures coming in unannounced and wrecking havoc."

"Wait a sec," she said, and spun to glare at him in a direct faceoff. "Are you saying that you being there had nothing to do with me?"

"That isn't exactly true."

She growled. "So why the telepathy?"

A grin spread across his face. The action transformed his features and he actually looked friendly.

For the first time she noticed his eyes were an incredible lucent green.

"Telepathy?" he asked. "Simple. I knew you'd

understand me. That's why the telepathy worked. The hounds didn't need to know I was there for you. Although they usually come well equipped with a strong sense of smell, very few have the gift of mind speaking."

"The tall guy couldn't smell magic."

Leeson shrugged. "He was still a hound and unwelcome in my city."

"So then..." Claire paused and chewed her lip. He was certainly a tough nut to crack. Not one for sharing information. She pressed him for the answer.

"You avoid my question of where you're from by stating this is your city. You mean to protect, right? Obviously, with that accent you weren't born here. Never heard a not quite Brit—twang before."

"That's a close enough guess-ta-ment."

"You know something? I don't like evasiveness." She planted her feet and glowered while waiting for an answer.

The vibrations coming from the earth fed inborn stubbornness. She could always borrow power from the earth. In this moment she did that with no qualms.

Claire circled her toe on the damp passageway floor marking the spot. "I'm not taking another step until you answer my question. How'd you find me in the park? Don't tell me you were there for the hounds. I don't believe you."

His jaw clinched. He watched her with narrowed eyes. Finally, he responded. "Earth magic?" Masculine fingers twitched around the wand. He lowered the tip toward the path. "She didn't say you have the gift of Insight."

Energy spiked up through the soles of Claire's old boots. "She? Insight? Why do you only give me more questions and no answers?"

The urge to kick him surfaced. Right there on the side of his knee. She could fell him like a mighty oak. Then flee, but that would have left too many unanswered questions.

"Relax," he said while putting his palm up to stop her. "*She* is the Colclough. It's my job to bring you in safely. She didn't tell me you have the gift of Insight."

He stopped speaking briefly while giving her a searching look. "Maybe she didn't know? Insight is just what it usually means. You have the ability to notice and understand things about a person that someone else will just blow off."

"Oh. I never considered that a gift."

"It's actually very powerful if one learns to manage Insight. Think of the truth you'll see."

She cleared her throat. "The Colclough?"

"Our clan oracle leader. She's been expecting you."

Claire huffed.

"You doubt the gift of foresight?"

"No," she replied. "I suppose not, but it's rather frustrating considering *I* don't know where to *expect* me."

His grin returned. "Well twirl around and climb that ladder. We're already late."

"Ugh. This new destination is really high."

"You didn't expect the Fault to be a tiny low rise crack in the earth, did you?"

The metal was cool against her palm. She wasn't convinced she wanted to climb. She stalled. "Fault?"

"As in San Andreas. This underground tunnel you've been walking in. Completely unknown to non-magical folk. Although the fault doesn't travel directly through the city, it serves as one magical portal to our destination."

She tilted her head and stared up into blackness. An odd sensation gripped her throat. She fought through the fear, and finally squeaked, "And exactly what destination is that?"

"Up the rungs and through a stone on your left."

"Wonder if I believe that one." She started climbing. "Heights," she muttered. If there was anything she truly didn't like, it was being high in the air. Give her the ground under her feet. A car or even a train was her idea of perfect traveling.

Claire climbed. Magical lights on either side of them lit the earthly shaft with just enough glow to see their direction.

Higher and higher up through the earth they journeyed.

After what seemed like fifty rungs, she stopped and looked down. "Whoa!"

Leeson's wand stuck from a loop on the back of his long coat. The tip lit the shaft.

Seeing how far they had climbed sent spikes of fear through all five senses. Her knees went weak.

She gripped the rung in front of her and took several breaths. The smell of earth soothed frazzled nerves.

Claire couldn't help but think of the old well behind the convent. There had been a legend about a young boy surviving a fall into the wet depths. She shivered as the memory passed through her thoughts.

"Nice view, isn't it?" Leeson's voice came up to her edged with laughter.

"You better not mean my butt!"

"Now that you mention it..."

She shoved her right foot downward. The only thing her foot found was the nothingness of empty air. Embarrassment made her flinch. The worn leather sole of her left boot slipped off the ladder rung.

"Ahhh!" Heart pounding, Claire realized her fingers were slipping. She kicked empty air. Fingers seeking something to grip scratched at the walls.

Panic!

"Easy."

Strong arms surrounded her.

She gasped and sputtered. Masculine scent filled her lungs. Words eluded while supercharged heat raced through her veins. The fabric of his coat was suddenly the dearest lifeline.

Heart pounding moments slipped by. "What are you standing on?" She experienced the vibration of his chuckle through layers of fabric.

"Air is my friend."

A groan eased from her lungs. The release calmed her rushing heart. "Piffle butt."

They floated upward.

"What's that mean?"

"Just something to replace swear words," she answered, still slightly breathless.

"Sister Teresa taught me. She understood that sometimes my emotions needed to be expressed. You know, because of magical buildup. If I didn't release my heightened feelings, that's when I'd get into trouble with accidental magic. So she taught me to release through words that sometimes were funny or unusual combinations."

"And here I thought you didn't like the nuns. I've already heard you swear."

"I loved Sister Teresa," Claire said low voiced. "She was my heart home during the darkest times of my life."

"Humm..." he said thoughtfully. "You know scars may remind us of our pain, but that doesn't mean they control where we're going. I'm sure she'd say the same thing."

His baritone voice soothed her. At first she didn't respond. Then with a soft sigh, she murmured, "She did say that. Just before she died."

"I'm sorry to hear that." He balanced her against the wall on a jutting ledge. "We've arrived."

She ducked her face, hiding a blush when his warm palm brushed the bare skin on her arm, and then pulled her toes back from the dangerous edge.

Leeson tapped a stone. The earth rumbled and began to split.

Several moments passed as magic adjusted the opening. A long elegant hallway appeared.

Patterned tile on the floor pointed the way.

The walls shifted gradually from earthly stone into beautiful, deep toned redwood paneling.

Elegant bronze sconces on both sides lit the passageway with welcoming ambiance. A massive circular doorway dominated the far end.

Even from this distance Claire saw deep staining in the carved surface. The artful design depicted a woodland grove and the creature inhabitants basking gleefully beneath a full moon.

Claire stood at the apex to an unknown future. From the second Leeson had spoken within her mind, she understood these moments in time were pivotal.

The patterned tile at her feet drew her in with whispers of magical certainty.

"You all right?" Leeson asked.

"Yes," she answered with a relieved sigh. "I

haven't felt this safe since I left the convent."

"Why did you leave?"

"It was time. Sister Teresa died just before my sixteenth birthday. The other sisters were wonderful, but they couldn't fill the empty spaces. I finished high school and left to see the world."

"That's when you discovered the magical dangers connected to your gifts?"

"You could say that. Sister Teresa tried to teach me that magical gifts are for the greater good. But the world away from her saw things differently. Especially when I was a kid."

"That's behind you now. Every step you take can change your future." He motioned toward the huge doorway. "Since the Colclough is expecting you, the doors won't open until you stand before them. Shall we go?"

"You have a nice smile," she said in response to his encouraging glance. "Try using it more often."

He revealed more teeth in a playful action and winked. "Sure. Maybe then I won't look like the typical protector of the innocent."

She snorted as she walked. "Some would say I've never been innocent. Come on slow poke. Let's meet the Colclough."

The sound of their footsteps lingered in echo behind them. Claire tried not to notice that the combination of her own and Leeson's footfalls mingled into an intriguing melody.

She refused to believe they could ever be more than friends.

However, the footstep melody wove around her heartstrings.

By the time they reached the circular door, she understood friendship with Leeson was already bigger than the massive facade now blocking their path.

"Who needs such huge doors?" she asked and resisted touching the intricate carving.

"Impressive, huh?"

She stared at the circular frame and sent eyes upward. "Must be twenty-five feet high. Wow."

"Obviously they've served their purpose. Extraordinary and daunting. Don't let the grandeur put you off. You are powerful in your own right. Click your heels."

"Excuse me?" She glared at him while disbelief shook her mind. "You're joking."

"Not just for faery tales. Go ahead. Give it a go."

She gazed at her scuffed and holey suede ankle boots. Ragged from her journey, they didn't measure up to ruby slippers or a glass pair either. The left boot even had a cut from an evil shape-shifter's claw. "Can't believe I'm doing this."

"Magic is boundless, you know."

"But faery tales?"

"Where do you think those stories came from? What is hidden in plain sight is frequently the most powerful." He motioned to her feet. "Waiting."

"Just great. I'll do it, but I better not end up in Kansas."

"San Francisco pyramid do?"

"Humph." Claire closed her eyes although she wasn't sure that was part of the spell. *Here goes.* She clicked three times.

"Atta girl."

"From now on don't come into my mind unless I invite you."

When Claire opened her eyes the doors split at the center and slid back into huge pockets. An opulent chamber welcomed her from across the threshold.

They were no longer underground. Magic had transported them to a penthouse in the sky.

Floor to ceiling windows displayed the panorama of San Francisco's nightscape. Her breath stopped completely while she studied the beauty. Then she focused on the woman standing in the middle of the room.

"Claire," Leeson said. "This is our highly esteemed Colclough."

"Welcome Claire," said the Colclough. "We've been expecting you." She was tiny and spoke in a soft voice. Leeson's muscular form next to the Colclough served as a size contrast; however, Claire had an impression of great power and strength surrounded by delicate blue fabric.

The Colclough's gown flowed as though the source of all air breathed through the cloth. A soft, silver French braid gave the small woman an aura of grand sophistication.

"Thank you," Claire said, and since she didn't know the correct protocol, she gave a slight curtsey. "Do you mind explaining how you knew I was coming?"

"That's very simple," the Colclough answered as she motioned toward a large circular table.

Claire approached and gazed down into a shiny surface. "Oh!" she said, breathless while seeing a replay of the battle in the park. "I've never seen such magic!"

"Your arrival was revealed to me six months ago. But I'm sure you are exhausted. Come with me, and you can settle into your room. We'll talk after you've rested."

They stepped through an archway and walked along a short hall. "Here you are." The Colclough gave her a smile and reached to touch her cheek.

"Peaceful dreams, my dear."

Warmth saturated Claire and fuzziness hugged the edge of her brain.

[2] *Fae Dreaming*

"Did you have to knock her out with a sleep spell?" Leeson asked as he looked down at Claire's peaceful countenance against his shoulder. She was light as a feather in his arms, and also molded to him in a perfect fit.

"I wasn't worried. Knew you would catch her." The Colclough pulled the coverlet back and plumped the pillow. "Put her on the bed."

He positioned Claire and stepped back just as gentle hands removed the worn out shoes.

"Bless her," she said. "When do you suppose she ever had a new pair? This one has two holes."

"Who knows? Wonder why she didn't just magic them."

"History," the Colclough said. "She uses her magic only when absolutely necessary. Comes from the horrible experiences in childhood. We'll teach her new ways."

Leeson brushed a stray black curl from Claire's cheek. "Is that really possible?"

"It's a necessity. Claire doesn't know yet, but her legacy is destined toward greatness." In slow motion, she passed hands six inches above Claire's sleeping form.

When she was finished, Claire wore a soft nightgown and looked fresh as if from a bath. "Time to let her rest. Come. I want to know about this pack of hounds."

Leeson followed her from the room.

Back in the antechamber, he strode to the closest window, and stared down at the view of San Francisco from the forty-ninth floor.

To the outside world the landmark pyramid was forty-eight floors. The best kept secret in Frisco was the power base on this hidden level. The Colclough kept watch over her magical domain from this sacred vantage point.

He shrugged out of his trench coat and held it at arm's length. With a brief thought the coat vanished into his chamber closet.

"You may lose the glamour if you like," Grace Colclough said.

"I am comfortable." She would always be Grace to him because he had known her since childhood.

"Claire won't wakeup if that's your concern. The sleep spell should last at least twenty-four hours or more."

"No. That isn't what's bothering me." He narrowed his focus to the reflection on the window glass. "I'll keep this face until the mission is complete. Maintaining the same magic without break will strengthen the bond between Claire and me."

"If you say so."

"I insist," he replied, and faced her. "The hounds tracked her too easily. Keeping the bond in place will shelter her even without my coat. That's what is more important."

"I noticed in the viewer you mentioned the lead hound was Grismere."

"I didn't recognize him until he exited. He has a particular vanishing point."

"Really? I didn't notice."

Leeson grunted. "Oh yes. He leaves a malodorous fart behind. Not a visual effect, but a distinctive one, none the less. Reeks. I remember an encounter with him some years ago in Cleveland. He's changed his face but not his signature."

Grace laughed. "Perhaps I should turn the scent application on the viewer to the receptive position. The function is shut off because frequently the air gets filled with too many outside aromas. But, if the odor's as bad as you say, I'll just take your word for it."

"Trust me; you don't want that smell blowing through this sacred place."

"Enough discussion then," she replied, and tilted her head toward the kitchen. "Would you like something to eat? I know it's been awhile since your last meal, and you'll need your strength while we figure out what to do about this latest threat."

"Food would be good. Protein if you have something."

Two quick claps and her manservant Miles appeared. "Yes, milady?"

"Lord Leeson is hungry. I'm sure he'd love some of the wild salmon and quinoa salad. Please bring extra lemon juice on the side."

"Of course," Miles said, and blended away with a stiff bow.

"Quinoa?"

"It's a super food. Fit for the gods," Grace explained. "Or even a Fae Mynwy."

"Humph. Whether one is referred to as Fae Mynwy or Prince, if one prefers that term, there is little difference with a man's appetite. It isn't necessary to paste the formalities on me. The need for food is all the same. You know that, Grace."

"Perhaps not," she replied. "However, I believe it's necessary to remind you of your station in life. I think you forget when you spend so much time this side of that magical veil. In Annwn's realm, you would be overseeing your own shire as Worthy Prince of Baderon."

"I haven't forgotten, but my current mission is important. It's on this side of the veil and one objective. Protect Claire. That's all there is."

She lowered long lashes to hide expressive eyes.

Something nagged at the back of his neck. He reached up and rubbed the queer sensation. "There's missing and important information you aren't telling me."

"Dinner is served," Miles said, and appeared bearing a huge silver tray.

"Thank you, Miles," Grace replied, and motioned toward a table, indicating Leeson should sit.

Miles made a big show of placing the plates in proper arrangement, but the actions didn't succeed in distracting him.

Leeson paused long enough for Miles to fade back to wherever he hid, and then he pushed. "I know there's something. Enlighten me."

She poured a glass of wine and passed it to him.

"Your silence is significant," he interjected. "It implies secrets." He raised the glass, swirled and sniffed. The fruity bouquet reminded him of home in Annwn. He sipped and allowed the flavor to fill his senses.

"Secrets," he repeated. "Just like you didn't tell me Claire has the gift of Insight."

"Does she?"

The wine went down the wrong pipe. He coughed, but still managed to glare. Then he returned the glass to the table with a deliberate action to imply determination.

"Funny thing," he growled roughly, throat still constricting from choking. He paused, cleared his throat, and then leveled his fiercest glare at Grace. "Claire said she doesn't like evasiveness. Now it's my turn to experience vagueness."

Leeson held her blue gaze for several moments, and then returned focus back to eating. He took a bite of salmon and paused to savor the richness. "Shall I wake her?" he asked while waving a forkful of tender pink fish. "Perhaps she could coax the answers we need from you."

The corner of Grace's mouth tucked up. "I don't believe you could. She's under a potent sleeping spell."

He placed his fork upon the plate and made to rise.

"All right," she said, and waved slender hands indicating he should stay seated. "That won't be necessary. Let her rest in peace."

She placed tiny feet on a plush ottoman with an air of relaxed casualness. "I've already told you Claire's legacy is destined for greatness."

He returned to his chair. "Vagueness. I'm waiting."

"I just told you."

"Piffle butt."

"What?"

"Just something our dear Claire likes to say." He quirked a brow. "Sister Teresa taught her. I figured since she was your *blood* sister you'd know the term."

Tears misted over Grace's eyes. "No. I try not to think of Teresa."

"So we're right back where we started. I don't believe you. You're hiding something, and I'm going to find out what it is. You're aware I will succeed."

"Well, I suppose you must know eventually anyway. My dear sister Teresa was put in place as

Claire's watcher." She arranged her skirt around her knees and fingered the blue cloth.

"The first time," she continued softly, "Teresa mentioned Claire was just before her death. I admit to being distressed that she'd never told me. I thought we were close. But Teresa revealed she'd been sworn to secrecy. She took that vow as seriously as the one she made to the church."

"Why appoint a watcher while Claire lived in the convent? Wasn't she already protected there?"

"Oh to be sure, she was."

Hushed moments rippled between them while each focused on their own thoughts.

Leeson broke the nuance of silence by clicking his fork on his plate. He pushed the food away. Only half finished, he had lost his appetite. He stood, and began pacing in front of the windows.

"I didn't tell you Claire's family name, did I?"

In front of the ottoman, he studied her cautious expression. "No. You didn't."

"Although Claire is an orphan, her grandsire still lives."

The hair on his arms rose. Leeson waited.

Grace's eyes dropped from his for a moment as though she considered how to put her next words together. At last, she returned focus, and said, "He endowed the convent with a small fortune in payment for her shelter."

"He abandoned her."

"Not precisely," Grace answered. "The plan was to keep her sheltered until the time was right. She graduated high school two weeks after her eighteenth birthday. Claire left the convent immediately without telling anyone."

Grace paused and studied him with focused directness. The sudden silence in the room made his heart pound in his ears.

Finally, Grace continued, "In the confusion of her disappearance she became truly lost. We've been looking for her ever since."

Leeson rubbed a hand over his arm. The last few minutes were unusual; experiencing two forewarnings in such a short period of time. First, the hairs on his neck fizzled, and now, the arm.

Bracing himself, he pressed for an answer. "You still haven't told me her family name. I'm assuming it's important since you're postponing any response I may have by withholding the information as long as possible."

Grace blinked and sat straighter. "Claire is Ayden Brinawell's granddaughter."

"That bastard!" he roared. "I told you she was abandoned!"

"Calm down."

"I will not!" He returned to pacing in front of the windows. With each step, anger grew in velocity. "If he didn't want her, he could've sent her Annwn." His voice cracked. "At least there, she would have grown up with all the privileges due to her station!"

"And her purpose would never have been fulfilled. She was protected and taken care of at the convent."

"That's ridiculous! Didn't you see her clothing and shoes? She nearly had a panic attack over losing a raggedy old blanket. That, and every time they tried putting her with a family, disaster struck. People in this realm didn't understand her magic."

Leeson stopped and stared at Grace. Her calmness did not appease the cyclone of fury battering his psyche. Planting his feet for grounding within this pyramid only increased the plethora of unexpected emotions. He needed air— the kind only flight would generate. But he would not leave until this situation was resolved.

Deep steady breaths began to ease him, but he remained rooted to the same place. Grace would have to reveal the secrets she kept. His determination, although silent and voiceless, was physical and potently magical.

Moments passed and he still refused to move; instead, he held her gaze like a hunter facing deadly prey.

"Your charm is powerful, but unnecessary, Leeson." She dropped her gaze. "You know about the prophecy?" she asked. "The one foretelling the uniting of the three houses of Annwn?"

"Yes," he answered. "Everyone knows about that. Sometime in the future, the three houses must unite because there's a great evil we'll need to defeat. It's said that only through blood union will that be possible."

"Claire is an important link to our future stability. Living here in the Earthly Realm was a requirement because this is where the threat will gain a foothold. I'm just grateful she's no longer lost."

"What you've said still doesn't excuse Brinawell abandoning her. Everyone knows he was furious when his son Alexander married an American witch."

"Allyssa wasn't just any witch," Grace remarked. "She was a Rockford."

"Didn't matter to Brinawell. He's a bastard. You won't convince me otherwise."

"Perhaps not," she remarked. "But I hope you don't lose your focus. We must see Claire safe no matter how you feel about her grandfather."

He stood next to the circular viewer where the conflict scenes in the park played in silent repetition.

It didn't matter that Brinawell was Claire's grandfather. She was already under his skin.

He knew the moment he caught her midair in the shaft that her magic harmonized his. Their power was equal and they mirrored each other with the perfection of a true match.

"I agree," he replied, paused the viewer playback and studied Grismere's face.

His magical sensors spiked. The sensation sharpened his focus on a small dark spot.

It was a mole, almost hidden in the scruffiness of three day beard growth, but suddenly blatantly obvious.

Not just any mole. Leeson scowled, tapped the viewer surface and pulled. The image zoomed in.

"What's wrong?" Grace asked.

He breathed through spiking adrenalin. "Bloody hell."

"Leeson?" She rose and moved toward him.

"Will Claire dream in her spell induced sleep?"

"Well yes," Grace answered. "That's why I specifically said peaceful dreams."

He tapped frantically at the viewer. "This isn't set to see Claire?"

"Of course. The purple bar."

He pressed. No response. He growled, spun on his heel, and ran through the arch leading to Claire's bedchamber.

"What's wrong?" Grace asked, while trying to keep pace with his long stride.

"Grismere has a dream catcher implanted on his cheek. That must be his plan B for tracking her if he can't pick up her scent."

Grace's eyes grew round with worry.

He shoved the chamber door open.

Claire lay in the center of her bed, eyes closed in blissful slumber.

All around her a dream grew into a hologram of color and light. Along the edges, semitransparent tendrils floated outward. Some extended to the walls and beyond.

"What a perfect beacon," he growled, and shook Claire, trying to wake her.

"That won't work," Grace snapped, while apprehension seeped from her pores.

He had never seen fear on the Colclough's face. Her expression magnified his anxiety. His mouth contorted, and he shouted, "Wake her!"

"The spell can't be broken. Magic must run its course." In a desperate move, Grace tried to cut through one of the tendrils as it escaped through the wall. "It was meant to protect her. Not this!"

"The wards!" he shouted. "Can Grismere get through the ward hiding this floor from the outside world?"

Grace paused in frozen frenzy. Her attempts to stop the dream tendrils expanding outward had failed. She stared around the room while visibly shaking.

Tense moments passed.

A harsh whisper finally came forth as Grace watched Claire's dream. "Can Grismere dreamwalk?"

His throat tightened. He didn't know.

Claire's dream kept building until the holographic images completely surrounded him with color. For the first time he wished for the ability to step into another's dreams.

"My God, Claire!" he yelled in his head. *"Wake up!"*

Laughter teased his mind.

"You can hear me?"

"Of course, silly," Claire answered, voice relaxed and edged with teasing.

"You've got to wake up. Grismere has a dream catcher implanted on his cheek. He's coming."

Leeson sat on the bed and held her hand. Claire's slender fingers entwined intimately with his.

Claire was silent although a soft smile crossed her features.

"Claire honey, listen to me."

She hummed within his mind. He thought the melody sounded familiar. Somehow, the tune renewed his urgency.

Soft black curls framed her face. The flush across her cheeks matched her deepening lip color.

He patted her cheek. *"Claire. Come back."*

She turned into his caress.

He groaned in desperation. A quick glance around them showed dream Claire dancing in a meadow bathed in sunshine. Laughter and singing. Flowers and tall grasses.

The simplicity of the scene made his heart pound. Would she ever return?

Dream Claire spun with her arms spread wide while fingertips added their own joyous rhythm. Her face tilted back, alabaster skin drank in the summer warmth.

"Leeson!" Grace yelled, and pointed.

He turned in the direction she indicated.

Grismere. A shadow of transparency, but there was no doubt the hound was coming for his prey. He had found access through one of the windows.

The dream tendril that the hound traveled on changed to a pulsating blood red hue.

The sight was sharp as a knife to his heart.

"Claire!" In an act of desperation he lifted her into his arms as his face fell.

Her soft lips yielded to his with the smoothness of a rose petal. He clutched her and tasted the sunshine on silky skin.

Claire's arms encircled him and he experienced a sensation of being pulled downward.

Pop.

Stunned, breathing in deep arousal, he stepped back and gazed into chocolate drop eyes. "What did you do?"

"We can share our mind, why not dreams?"

"You've got to wake up," he repeated while glancing around at the dream. "Grismere's traveled here on a dream catcher."

An animalistic roar disrupted their peace.

Claire's small hand slipped into his. She pulled hard. The unexpected momentum ripped them through the dream edges.

They landed on the Persian rug next to the bed.

Leeson's lungs collapsed due to the unexpected magical shift. He struggled to stand, but could only gasp desperately in need of air, and observe the pending attack with dread.

Above them, Grismere's holographic form charged toward Claire with a ferocious growl. Mouth opened wide, yellowed fangs exposed a grotesquely pierced tongue.

Claire's hands shot upward and snapped together. The remainder of dream energy vanished.

"Bloody hell." He gave up trying to stand and plopped back on the rug.

The reek from a gassy dog fart pillowed in the air.

| Part Two |
Perfect Match
Tears are not the mark of weakness,
but of power.
Washington Irving

* * * * * * * * *

[3] Insights of the Heart

"Well, I never expected *that*," the Colclough said. She stood next to Leeson and gazed between him and Claire with avid curiosity.

Claire suddenly realized she was sitting on the floor in a nightgown that brushed her skin with soft sexiness.

Heat rushed through her veins. She scrambled to stand even as she noticed Leeson staring at her thighs with unexpected fixation.

"My jeans! Where are they?"

"Oh not to worry, my dear," the Colclough explained, "I magiced them away when we tucked you into bed."

"We?" Shock pierced her brain. Claire stared at Leeson's rakish grin and mussed hair. She had created those tangled strands with tingling fingers during their dream inspired kiss.

Emotions enflamed, she straightened, pivoted and showed him her back.

"Please magic my clothes back," she said while trying to control wobbly knees. "I'd like to get dressed."

Lifting her chin, she headed for the closest door hoping in fierce stubbornness that it was a bathroom.

Safely on the other side, the oak paneled door was the only barrier between her and that infuriating man. Okay, so she had begun to think they could be friends just before they arrived, but that didn't excuse him being so forward now.

She rubbed her forehead hard and stepped in front of the sink. A mirror revealed all her secrets.

Arousal flushed her cheeks. The look in her eyes. She gasped. *Dewy? Oh my god!* Even her lips blushed a deep berry color with a remembered kiss.

The heartbeat in her chest sang with new discovery. *Oh Claire... we are in trouble.*

Someone knocked. "Are you all right?"

Claire closed her eyes, blocking the resulting sight from her amorous linking with Leeson. "Yes, ma'am."

"I have your clothing, dear. You may shower if you wish, but I did clear you magically before we left you to sleep."

There was that *we* word again. She released a sigh. "Thank you. I think I will shower. Please leave my clothes on the bed."

"Of course," the Colclough said. "Take your time. The sun is just rising. When you're ready, breakfast will be served."

"All right. Thanks. I just need..." Claire paused and gazed at her reflection again. "Some time."

A hot shower revived her enough to face the world. She stepped into the bedroom and discovered everything had been tidied. Fresh clothing lay on the silk duvet.

She fingered the denim jeans, smoothed the lightweight short sleeved sweater and eyed the new suede boots. Everything was identical to what she had worn before, but they were brand new and still had tags hanging from them. Even the under garments were new.

She found scissors in the nightstand drawer and used them to remove the tags.

Claire began dressing. When she finished, she noticed her driver's license and a few dollars on the nightstand. She pocketed them and sat to pull the boots on.

The old boots had been a half size too big. Purchased at a second hand shop she had accepted that imperfection.

The new pair fit perfectly. Blue suede, soft to the touch, hugged her ankles with just the right amount of support. She stood in front of the mirror and combed her wet hair.

"Stop procrastinating," she muttered to her reflection. "Time to go and figure out what's next."

Brilliant sunshine soothed the remembered hallway with heart touching warmth. She followed the sound of voices.

"That's how it is, Leeson," the Colclough said. "They must be notified. We can't let Grismere get the upper hand."

"I'm not saying let Grismere get the advantage," Leeson replied. He lounged casually against the viewer with manly confidence. "All I'm saying, we need to find a way to stop him that doesn't involve— Oh. Good morning, Claire."

"Doesn't involve what?" Claire asked.

His expression shifted to a mask of secrets, and he glanced quickly at the Colclough.

"Nothing to fret about, my dear," the Colclough said. "Leeson is already spending too much energy worrying."

Leeson moved away from the viewer, growled and bristled with visible stubborn demeanor.

"We've got to stop the dream catcher," he insisted. "You know that."

Claire leaned forward and studied Grismere's face in the misty surface of the magical viewer. "The spot on his cheek? Is that what you were talking about earlier?"

"Yes," Leeson replied, and pointed to emphasize the importance of the dark mark on Grismere's face. "It's a dream catcher. He must have gotten the spell and skin graft from a powerful sorcerer. Most likely someone connected to the Sable Thorne Brethren."

"What's the Sable Thorne Brethren?"

"They're a branch of the Chamber of Shadows which is the ruling house of Hades.

"The base of operations is called the Cliffmonte Manor. They're located on a bluff overlooking the River Styx. They're a multileveled cadre of wickedness which also happens to be well funded."

"Whoa. Slow down," Claire stated and held her palms facing him. There was already confusion in her mind and this new information added to her bewilderment.

"Remember," she continued. "I'm new to this. You're saying this Sable Thorne Brethren is a secret organization located by the River Styx? The mythical river?"

Leeson coughed into his hand, obviously hiding a laugh.

"My question is funny?" she asked, and crossed arms over her chest.

"Well, not that funny," Leeson said. "It's more surprising that with your gift of Insight you don't realize the truth. The River Styx isn't a myth. It circles the underworld nine times."

"I always believed the River Styx was just a scare tactic the nuns taught us so we'd behave."

"Oh, it's scary all right," he remarked. "Each member of the Chamber of Shadows must swear an oath upon the River Styx's holiness and be baptized in the waters. The Sable Thorne Brethren, the uppermost level of power, is equivalent to an earthly realm's high priest. The Brethren's influence spreads seamlessly between earth and Hades."

She shivered. "An oath? What sort of oath?"

"A fealty oath," he answered. "You know what that is?"

"Of course," Claire answered.

"The River Styx oath strengthens their power." He nodded, extended his palm toward her and quirked a brow. "Their main mission is to seek out those who bring light into the world and destroy them."

"Light?"

"Good magic, healing and helping others. If you doubt they are real there's something you should know. The Sable Thorne Brethren were involved in the most famous murder in history."

He tilted his head and paused while she absorbed that statement. Then he added with emphasis, "Think thorns."

Claire sucked her lower lip in and chewed. "Thorns?"

He nodded.

Realization sank in. "Oh...oh my god!"

Leeson leaned back against the viewer. "Precisely."

"So now they've singled me out," Claire said, while struggling to breathe. She inhaled a ragged breath and released the air with one determined push.

"Because of my good magic?" The words came out in a screech and strained her throat. She fought the painful sensation, and asked, "And that hound faced mutt actually tracked me to the park through a dream?"

"Were you dreaming when you were there?" the Colclough asked. She wore a crease between perfectly shaped brows.

Claire still wasn't accustomed to the Colclough's delicate serenity, but she realized the frown wasn't a frequent expression.

Comprehending such a small fact about the Colclough fed the nervous butterflies that already flitted in Claire's belly.

Claire hated admitting the reoccurring nightmare had visited during troubled sleep in the park. Exhaustion always brought that visual horror to the forefront of her subconscious.

Finally, after long soundless moments filled with their concerned glances, she spoke.

"There's a nightmare," she whispered. The words clogged in her throat. She placed fingertips at the base of her neck. The action allowed warmth to penetrate and calmed discomfort away.

Revived, she continued. "The bad dream always visits when I'm very tired or stressed."

"Visits?" Leeson asked. "That's a strange way to refer to a dream."

"That's because my dreams are different from the average person. Didn't you realize that when you were trying to wake me?"

He made hand motions in the air. "You mean the holographic energy surrounding you while you dreamed?"

"Precisely," Claire answered. "Sister Teresa always told me that energy was there when I dream because I actually visit myself at different times of my life. So, in my nightmare, I'm seven years old and reliving an abusive encounter."

She stopped speaking and stared at the hound faced stalker in the viewer. "Now, you're saying this mutt knew about my dreams and is chasing me through them. How did he know?"

Leeson shrugged. "Maybe an informant. Perhaps at the convent?"

"No!" Claire insisted. She refused to believe one of the nuns could betray her in such a personal level. "That's not possible! The sisters wouldn't tell anyone."

"It's going to be all right," the Colclough said. "We can work through this. You aren't alone anymore."

"I didn't mean to imply the informant was one of the Sisters," Leeson said gently. "There's other possibilities you may not be aware of."

Claire shook her head and rubbed fingers hard on her forehead. The action was a habit from her early teens. She had heard the pressure and movement increased blood flow to the frontal lobe.

Right now, she wasn't so sure because it felt like all the blood had drained from her head. A tiny seed of uncertainty fed the butterflies in her belly. They multiplied at an uncomfortable and sickening rate.

"How can we stop him?" she asked. "I'm... Well, I dream a lot. As in, drop off to sleep and pop into dreamland. Fast, consistently and never a break from routine."

"Simple," the Colclough answered. "Now that we realize Grismere can travel upon your dreams, we'll have to halt them temporarily."

"I know I asked before, but how? Dreams are dreams. No one thinks of being vulnerable while they're sleeping." Claire tried to stop the shaking that now ruled under her skin. She blamed the hyper butterflies that wanted to escape her belly.

This whole situation presented a new found danger. One she wasn't prepared to handle. "Besides, Sister Teresa always said dreams are a part of a healthy life. Even the nightmares."

"That's true," the Colclough remarked. "We'll only put a temporary stop to them. I can mix a potion that will filter your dreams into a safe container. An artifact perhaps or even your pillow might suffice. That way, you won't actually be losing the essence of the dreams and our actions will protect, but won't affect your health."

Claire stepped away from the viewer and stumbled to a soft chair. Comfy fabric and cushions caught her in time. There was no hiding the shaking from Leeson and the Colclough now.

"Bless you," the Colclough said softly. "It must be because you're hungry. Miles, come please."

The manservant stepped through the closest bookcase. "Yes, milady?"

"That breakfast I requested. We are ready now."

"Of course," he responded, and blended away.

Claire stared at the place he vacated. "Who?"

Leeson caught her confused glance. She experienced a surge of gratitude. He was the most familiar relationship in this strange new world.

"That's just Miles," he explained, and waved toward the hallway. "He does odd things around here for Grace. Should be back in a moment with food."

"Grace?" Claire glanced between them.

"My given name, dear. Leeson takes liberties, but I don't mind. Especially since I can tell you about him when he was just a tot. If it makes you more comfortable, you may call me Grace, too."

"Breakfast is served," Miles said, and then appeared. He held a French blade knife with a fancy wooden handle. Sunlight coming through the windows glistened upon the blade.

Claire flinched.

Miles winked at her and tapped the oval conference table. Glitter zoomed from the tip of the knife and hovered above the table. When the small, shiny particles floated downward and landed upon the mahogany surface, dishes and scrumptious looking food appeared.

A wondrous aroma filled the room.

"Oh my," Claire whispered in awe.

Leeson laughed. "He's just showing off."

"Who cares. Let's eat." Claire rose from the chair. "Thank you, Miles. You are my hero."

Miles gave her a deep bow. "Anytime, miss." He vanished with a gentle flutter of air.

"About this hero thing," Leeson said while holding a chair away from the table for her.

"Humm?" She sat, placed a napkin on her lap and studied the food selection spread across the table.

She wanted to tease him by pretending to ignore him, even though she sensed his need to talk about the altercation at park and the subsequent dream.

"Categorize heroism for me?" Leeson said. "You know, does fighting vicious hounds count? In being a hero, I mean? Perhaps waking you from a perilous dream with a rousting kiss?"

"Food. Right now, providing food is top of my hero list." She hid her face in a luscious glass of very cold milk. *Simply delicious.*

Of course, sudden shyness could also have something to do with the flutter around her heart caused by his utterly perplexed expression.

She set the glass down, and tapped her mouth with the napkin, hiding a smile. That's when she noticed Grace eyeing Leeson over half moon reading glasses.

Where'd those glasses come from? Ah, there's a newspaper next to Grace's plate.

"Hem hem..." Grace uttered while giving Leeson a speculating glance.

Claire had the impression Grace was teasing Leeson, too.

"Don't let her fool you, Claire," Leeson remarked. "Grace doesn't need those glasses. They are a profound fashion statement."

"Well, they are pretty," Claire commented as she buttered a slice of cinnamon toast.

"Thank you," Grace replied. "Would you like some blackberry preserves?"

"It's uncanny," Claire said while she took the crystal serving jar. "That you know what I like."

"I must honestly tell you," Grace whispered, and gave Claire a sad smile while moisture welled in deep set sapphire eyes. She paused a moment to compose herself, and then continued in a stronger voice, "Before we go any further; you must know, Sister Teresa was my blood sister."

Claire gasped. The spoon slipped from her fingers, and she reached for the Colclough's hand.

"I knew she had a sister. One she was very close to. I'm sorry for your loss."

"Thank you, my dear. She spoke of you with great love. However, I didn't fully understand at the time."

"Understand?"

"She never had children of her own. When you arrived at the convent and they placed you in her care, she fell in love. Each time you were shuffled to a foster home she mourned. Hours she spent in prayers and contrition. You always came back to her."

Tears burned Claire's cheeks. She wiped at them with her napkin, but the heat remained. "When I was smaller I didn't realize the Reverend Mother insisted I be placed in a foster home. Then, in my early teens, my goal was to get back to the convent so I wouldn't be leaving Sister Teresa."

Grace smiled through sadness. "She suspected as much."

"Well, it was easy. Use magic. Freak the family out and whoosh! Back to the convent. My shortest foster family stay set a record at an hour and a half. Ninety minutes from arrival to boot out."

Leeson shook his head in obvious disgust.

"Blaming them doesn't do much good now, Leeson," Claire replied. "I take responsibility for my actions, even if I was a kid." She picked up her teacup and placed delicate porcelain in her left palm. "If you didn't know or believe in magic, what would you think about this?"

She activated the magical energy in her palm and fingers. The cup rose above her hand and began to spin in slow motion.

Leeson tilted his head and studied the magical action. "That depends."

"On what?" Claire asked.

"If they could see the magical particles swirling or they thought you were doing a parlor magician's levitation trick."

Grace shook her newspaper and came from behind the pages. "What magical particles? I only see the cup levitated two inches above Claire's hand."

Claire froze. "You can't see the micro particles between my hand and the teacup?"

"No," Grace answered and leaned closer. "There's a bit of a glow, but no particles."

"Is it common for people to see them?" Leeson asked. "I've never seen someone's magic so distinctly."

"Sister Teresa saw the particles as faery glimmer. At least that's what she called them."

She set the cup back on the table. "When I see the particles, I also see the energy movement. The point I'm trying to make is, if someone was unaccustomed to magic and they witnessed this little trick, their usual reaction was to send me packing. Using magic worked every time after I turned eleven."

Leeson took a bite of his toast. "Still no excuse," he muttered.

Claire shrugged and decided it was time to focus on eating.

The quiet around the table as they ate gave a soothing aura to the chamber. Leeson finished first and broke the silence by shoving his chair away from the table.

Claire pushed the last bite of her eggs around on the plate. She was full and hesitated leaving them uneaten. "Everything was delicious. Thank you. I haven't eaten such wonderful food since I left the convent."

"That was more than a year ago," Leeson said. "How have you been eating since then?"

"Mostly food kitchens."

Leeson made a grumbling sound in his throat.

"Every so often I wait tables," Claire said. "That gives me some cash to get by. Sometimes diner owners feed the help."

Unexpected warmth blossomed her in the chest. Claire touched her gold locket, and brought it out of the hidden magical pocket realm. The gold warmed her fingertips.

What's going on? Claire wondered.

"Is something wrong?" Grace asked.

Leeson eyed the locket.

"My goodness," Grace commented. "What a pretty necklace. I didn't notice you wearing jewelry before."

"That's because I concealed it magically," Claire explained. "Wearing gold and traveling alone is a dangerous combination. The gold just heated up. Sometimes that happens and I don't always know why."

"It must be a powerful artifact," Grace replied. "Where did you get it?"

Claire held the locket dangling on a delicate chain. The little heart spun and glistened in the sunshine. "The Reverend Mother gave it to me. She told me Sister Teresa had been saving this locket for my eighteenth birthday. There are two pictures inside. One of my parents and the other is a toddler picture of my mom."

The look on Grace's face changed dramatically. "Well isn't that fascinating?"

"Why bring your locket out now?" Leeson asked.

Claire shrugged. "I just had a warm tingling sensation from the gold. Guess you could say sometimes the locket alerts me."

She palmed the locket, wrapped fingers around warmth, and tried getting a better magical read from its golden vibration.

"But it doesn't always do that?" Leeson asked. "I mean at the park. Did the locket warn you then?"

"No, it didn't," Claire answered. "I admit, I don't always understand. But it warmed just now."

"Perhaps," Grace remarked as she folded the newspaper and rose from her chair, "that's because Katrina is coming up the elevator."

"You have an elevator?" Claire asked, and glanced around the room.

"Of course, my dear," Grace answered. "We're very modern here, you know."

"Rina's coming?" Leeson's face paled.

In fact, Claire thought Leeson had the nervous appearance of a bird in a cage, grateful for the wires separating him from a nasty old cat.

Grace laughed and waved a hand in nonchalant dismissal. "Relax Leeson. She won't bite. I won't let her." The humor in her eyes multiplied.

Leeson bristled visibly and scowled. Broad shoulders stiffened as he stood straighter.

"She'll have information for us," Grace answered. "You know she's been places you'd never journey."

"Humph."

Claire bent forward. "What's—"

She didn't finish because the bookcase sliding outward snapped her to attention. Standing in the center of the elevator was the largest black cat Claire had ever seen.

The cat moved with lissome paw steps and approached Grace. The bookcase slid closed and melded seamlessly back into the wall.

Grace tickled the cat's ears. "Please transform, Katrina. You're making Leeson nervous," she said with laughter lacing through her voice.

Claire's only experience with a shapeshifter had been a bad one; on the level of a near death experience.

She braced herself and watched in trepidation as the cat moved upright and eventually revealed a woman of undeterminable age with smooth porcelain pale skin marked with Celtic styled lines painted across her forehead.

The woman's gaze locked with Claire's.

Moments passed as Claire stared into expressive cat eyes. Then, in slow motion, the eye color gradually changed to a mellow hazel and pupils softened to circular darkness.

"You know I won't harm you," Katrina said with a purring lilt. She nodded toward Claire's locket. "Your totem speaks wisdom. Listen to it now. Let the locket reveal truth."

"How did you know," Claire asked, "that my locket heated to notify me of your arrival?"

Katrina touched the cat collar around her neck. While in human form, the necklace was fashioned from black beads. At the center, an onyx heart hung on a small gold ringlet.

"Because," Katrina answered in a silky voice. "Once I stepped onto the elevator, mine told me you had arrived safely in this sacred shelter. If you listen to yours, the magic will keep you safe."

"I'll work on that. Thanks," Claire replied. "Grace mentioned you go places Leeson won't. Why?"

Katrina laughed. She winked at Leeson and pulled a chair away from the conference table. "Grace just means I'm a little closer to the ground. I also spend time in the alleys, fresh air markets and along the docks."

"What have you heard," Grace asked, and poured Katrina a glass of milk.

"Thank you," Katrina said as she took the refreshment. "Whispers aren't good." She drank deeply, and then placed the glass on the table.

Leeson sat, but leaned backward in the padded chair as though keeping his distance. "When are whispers ever good? Have you heard anything about who's after Claire? We thought the Chamber of Shadows was responsible."

"That's the least of your problems...*now*," Katrina remarked while she studied him through narrowed eyes.

Voices collided in the air.

"Least?" Claire asked.

"What's that mean?" Leeson asked sarcastically.

"Hem hem," Grace uttered. "Why don't we give Katrina a chance to explain?"

Katrina stretched her arms upward and her legs under the table. She wiggled her middle and then pulled legs up under her bottom while snuggling against the padded chair back. "Smartest words I've heard all day," she replied.

"Please," Claire said, and tried to control the emotion in her voice. "Explain why the Chamber of Shadows is the *least* of my problems?" Claire paused and stared into Leeson's eyes.

The sense of safety Claire had experienced since arriving at Grace's home suddenly had a foreshadowing effect hanging in the tense air around the conference table.

"Is..." Claire winced when her voice cracked. "Is there really something worse than the Chamber of Shadows?"

"There is now," Katrina said.

Grace sat in the chair next to Katrina. "Yes, please tell us what you've heard."

Katrina looked at each of them for long moments. Finally, she stopped at Leeson. "There was a death in the park. Do you know the man's name? The one that died?"

"No," Leeson answered. "I was battling two hounds and didn't ask their names."

"He was a daemon," Claire said. "The hellion cleaners took him. I saw them devour his remains."

Katrina faced Claire. "Yes, he may have been a daemon. That just makes the situation worse."

"How?" Claire experienced prickly spikes poking under the skin. The sensation was hyper nervousness, she knew, but that acknowledgement didn't make the anxiety vanish.

"Because he had a brother," Katrina replied with a matter-of-fact tone.

"So?" Leeson's brows shot downward and furrows deepened across his forehead.

"I realize you're not getting the ramifications, Lee," Katrina snapped sharply.

"Leeson," he growled back at her with bared teeth.

"Stop your quarreling," Grace interrupted. "Why are this dead daemon and his brother so special?"

Katrina spoke with sharp crispness. "The dead daemon was Dante Marchosias."

Realization hit and Leeson gasped.

"That's right," Katrina said. "The youngest Marchosias. His elder brother Weyer wants you dead, displayed *and* ravaged on a spike located specifically on the banks of the River Styx. A trophy of revenge so everyone can see what happens when a fae murders a daemon."

"What's a Marchosias?" Claire asked.

"The Marques of Hades," Leeson answered. "A Fallen of the worst sort."

"Fallen? Oh," Claire said. "You mean a fallen angel. They became daemons. There's actually a marquis in Hades?"

"Several, in fact," Grace answered. "Katrina, I get the impression you're blaming Leeson for this death. Surely you realize he was following my instructions. Our goal is to protect Claire."

"I understand that," Katrina said. "You must know that now this situation won't be easy. For years the Marques ignored the Chamber of Shadows insistence that Claire must be captured. Now that his brother is dead, Marquis Weyer's aura of vengeance will spread as a bloody virus into his legions. They'll be vicious."

Grace closed painted eyes, and reclined her head on the back of the chair. Silver eyelashes laced softly across lined cheeks. Even in stillness an aura of mystical energy swirled around her. The energy spread through the quiet chamber atmosphere like a sacred prayer.

They waited with bated breath for the insight Grace would reveal. The blue fabric of her gown stirred upon the softly moving air.

When she opened eyes they had the

appearance of sapphire gems with no white showing. Her voice vibrated with steeliness. "We must face this marquis. The quicker the better. If vengeance infects his legions, they will outnumber us and we won't be able to stop them."

"I agree," Katrina said.

"We'll have to draw him out," Leeson said as he studied Claire.

Outside, a cloud passed in front of the San Francisco sun. The room dimmed.

Claire shivered. In her mind, the heavenly movement on the other side of the window was a shadowy omen. One she didn't like.

"The Marques of Hades is already earthside," Katrina stated with calculated resolve.

"How do you know?" Leeson's face took on an expression of ruthlessness, one Claire had not seen.

Katrina's cheeks and nose shifted as though she twitched whiskers at Leeson's question. "I've been in the thick of wicked conversation. Cats can do that."

"If you're sure, then we must prepare," Grace replied. She rose from the chair and moved toward the viewer.

"Wait a minute," Claire said. "I'm still hung up on the *draw him out* issue. Leeson, why are you looking at me like that?"

Outside, the cloud moved on its journey across the sky. Sunshine burst through the windows and slanted across the room with renewed vigor.

"What are you thinking?" Claire asked Leeson while rubbing her hands together. She hoped opening her magic during these stressful moments would help her cope.

Leeson shook his head, shoved shirt sleeves up strong forearms, and stopped in front of the viewer. "I was unaware of that hound's identity. But, I wouldn't change what happened. They were there to kill you."

Gooseflesh twitched along her arms. Claire rubbed her skin and used hand magic to stave off the physical reaction.

"Thank you for saving my life," Claire said. "Why do I get the impression you're about to request something scary? This is one of those times when an incomplete Insight can be unnerving."

"They want you," Leeson said in a matter-of-fact tone edged with purpose. "I think we should give false information about your location and then wait for them to attack."

She inhaled a long slow breath while gazing into his eyes.

No one spoke. They waited for her response.

Finally, Claire nodded. "Not to be pushy, but I'll only agree if everyone is careful. I don't want anyone getting hurt on my account."

"That's doable," Katrina said.

Leeson placed palms flat on the table top. "Let me be clear," he insisted with steely determination. Every muscle in his body roared with magical tenacity while he stared at Katrina. "The information about Claire's location will be completely false."

"Leeson." Claire wanted to break through his ferociousness.

"Is that clear, *Rina*?" he asked and leaned closer to make his point.

"Crystal," Katrina said. "You don't have to convince me otherwise."

"Leeson," Grace urged firmly. "Give up your preconceived notions. You shouldn't doubt Katrina's sincerity. She wants to help."

An unexpected urge rose in Claire. She touched his arm and eased ruffled male emotions with gentle magic. "You said I have Insight. Do you believe that?"

He caressed the inside of her wrist with a feather soft touch, and then took her hand. Their fingers entwined intimately while he gazed into her heart and soul.

Gentle strength emanated in his tender expression.

That was how she saw him; a fiercely protective warrior, and a man not quite ready to admit the sensations journeying though their joined hands.

She placed her other hand over his heart. "Do you believe?" she asked while his breathing and pulse increased.

"Yes," he murmured.

"Then believe I can *see* that Katrina is here to help."

His emotionally facetted eyes did not blink.

She leaned nearer and allowed his breath to whisper longing across her skin. "Please," she said low, the word meant only for him.

His strong fingers combed through her hair. Never before had she experienced such an intimate joining than these precious moments.

Heart pounding, Claire knew their closeness supercharged the mood in the room. She surrendered to the intimate potency and brushed his lips with eagerness.

A deep groan and Leeson returned the kiss with heady urgency.

Claire allowed his kiss to consume every doubt and build a blushing foundation of future potential.

After long moments she drew back.

"Well that was interesting," Katrina remarked. "Definitely a unique way to change the subject."

Leeson placed his forehead against Claire's. "Subject isn't changed. I still don't trust you, but I trust Claire completely. Her word is my bond."

"That's settled then," Grace stated in a relieved tone. "We'll have to plan carefully. Claire, I believe the first place to start is your necklace."

Claire fingered the gold locket in puzzlement. "My necklace?"

"Yes, my dear. The locket's perfect," Grace replied. She approached one of the tall bookcases and ran fingers along colorful bindings. She spoke softly as though whispering to the books.

Claire heard the murmuring but not specific words. "Are all your books about magic?" She thought she saw a small book move on the shelf by itself.

"Oh, no dear," Grace answered, still focused on her book quest.

"Even if a book isn't about magic," Leeson replied, "that doesn't mean there's no magic connected to its history."

"Ah, there you are," Grace commented as she tilted her head back. She reached a hand toward the top shelf.

Claire watched in amazement as the shelves moved downward, magically compacting until the book Grace needed could be retrieved.

"This should have the perfect potion," Grace remarked, and placed *The Shadow Seeker's Guide to Esoteric Potions* on the table. She opened the elegant black and green cover and began flipping pages.

"I still don't understand," Claire said. "You're going to make a potion and use my necklace?"

She clutched the gold. "Will the potion ruin it?"

"Of course not," Katrina said. "Grace wants to use the magic of your locket to help protect you. No, there won't be any damage."

Claire still hesitated even though she realized that Katrina's smile was meant to reassure.

"Using the locket," Katrina said, "will increase your magic by connecting you on a deeper magical level with your family. The gold is already a powerful totem on its own."

"But I don't have any family," Claire said.

Leeson covered his mouth while he coughed.

She frowned at him as furtive glances passed among everyone.

"Not to worry," Grace remarked, and continued turning pages. "The energetic magic of the former owner still resides within the locket. Gold does that."

"Does what?" Claire asked, still confused.

This morning had already revealed many new spectrums of magic. It was difficult to take in so much information in rapid succession. But Claire understood the basic necessity. *Just one step at a time, please.*

Leeson moved forward and touched the delicate chain. "Since gold comes from the earth it carries magical properties." The sound of his voice played along her skin in a soft caressing resonance. "I'm sure you've heard of crystal magic. Well, most folk overlook the potential of gold magic."

Claire dangled the heart away from her chest and let it spin. She loved doing that because the light caught the diamond center of the engraved star and sparkled. "So you're saying this locket is infused with my mother's magic?"

"Precisely," Katrina said.

"We'll tweak the magical energy a little," Grace commented with a quirked brow, "and then it'll be perfect."

Lines formed around Leeson's eyes as surprise traced high cheekbones. "Tweak?" he asked, and shifted his gaze between Claire and Grace.

"Certainly," Grace answered briskly without looking up from her reading. "Katrina, do me a favor and get the hourglass, cauldron and some blessed thistle from the garret room."

Katrina headed toward a door that moved into view when the fireplace slid to the left side.

"Leeson." Grace passed fingertips over a list on the page. "We'll need your crystal dagger."

The corners of his full lips tucked up and he snapped his fingers. An ivory hilted dagger wrapped in a black leather sheath appeared on the table next to Grace's book.

"Thank you," Grace replied, finally glancing up from reading.

Katrina arrived, arms filled with several odd items. "I know why you need the small cauldron, blessed thistle and I brought the portable stand for the cauldron. But why do we need an hourglass?"

Claire fingered the miniature jar that contained blessed thistle. "May I ask, how did Leeson just snap his fingers and a dagger appeared from someplace, but Katrina went upstairs to get this stuff?"

"First, to answer Katrina's question," Grace replied. "The sands of time from the hourglass will assist us toward our goals." She pulled a pouch from a pocket hidden in the folds of her blue dress.

After unzipping the small bag, Grace opened the soft fabric, and then removed several pearl handled metal instruments. The pearl handles were embellished with a painted floral design.

With quick efficient movement, Grace arranged the tools in a neat line next to the herbs and hourglass. The last item she pulled from the pouch was a matching porcelain vial with a purple screw on top.

"As for the difference between Leeson's magic," Grace answered while indicating the resealed doorway to the garret. "The items I asked Katrina to bring down were in a room upstairs which has a powerful protective ward. It's simply a necessary precaution."

"The garret ward is a second line of defense," Leeson remarked. "Even though this whole floor is hidden from the outside world by an obscurity ward, the garret is an inner sanctum with additional security."

"This floor is hidden?" Claire asked.

"Yes," Grace answered while opening the jar of dried blessed thistle. She spread some of the herb in the bottom of the cauldron. Fingering the dried herb until she was satisfied with its arrangement, she paused and then reached for a small vial that she had taken from the pouch. "This lavender essential oil will help the spell."

Grace tipped the small bottle, waited until two drops of lavender landed on the dried blessed thistle, and then twisted the cap back on. She stirred the oil into the dried herb and blew a gentle breath across the surface.

"Claire," Grace murmured. "Please put your locket on the blessed thistle here in the center of the cauldron. Open it so we may see the pictures."

As she spoke, Grace loosened the top of the hourglass. The granules had already begun falling into the bottom portion with quickening speed.

Claire removed the locket and spread the little hearts open. She placed the gold charm carefully in the cauldron.

The room became quiet as everyone focused on observing the sands of time slipping by in a flowing vortex.

In an ephemeral movement, Grace flicked nimble fingers.

Time stopped.

Claire gasped.

Three granules of sand remained in perfect suspension in the center of the narrowest point of the hourglass.

Outside of paused time, Grace reached for a set of long tweezers and moved with delicate precision into the glass container.

"We must all center our intention," Grace intoned. "Think only of protecting Claire in your own particular method."

A surreal sensation fluttered in airy lightness over Claire's skin. She experienced seeing time frozen, but there was movement when Grace plucked each granule and placed them individually into the opened locket.

The simple actions had profound and powerful effects on Claire.

When the first hourglass sand granule landed upon the image of Claire's dead parents a warming sensation starburst from Claire's heart. It was an opening of love that shook her to the foundations of her soul.

The second time granule opened her mind to the sound of long gone parental voices. They spoke without the use of words, but she knew them on a visceral level. There was no doubt, only pure and certain knowledge of their presence.

Tears flowed freely from Claire's eyes. She could not have stopped them even if she wanted.

Claire understood the flow of lost life and love came directly from her parents Alexander and Allyssa Brinawell.

The frequency of parental love hugged with powerful angelic wings. Claire realized their love frequency had been with her each and every moment throughout her life.

The newfound acknowledgement changed Claire's awareness to a unified connection with her dead parents.

The third sand granule touched her mother's toddler picture. A disruptive cry of anguish escaped from Claire. She went to her knees while tears increased.

The linked magic between Claire and her parents grew in frequency and potency with each shed tear.

Tears flowed as though a river.

Time continued in the chamber outside Claire's immediate consciousness.

However, within her personal aura, Claire knew only the purest vibration of absolute love. That power of love formed a holographic violet flame around her body.

The magical flame sheltered Claire within a shimmering veil of ethereal movement, and tickled until the magic settled into an iridescent, semisolid bubble.

Claire rose to unsteady feet, blinked back the moisture in her eyes, and tried to see the room outside the bubble.

In an unexpected move, the bubble rose into the air and spun in a vortex of electrical energy. The movement mesmerized Claire as energy wove in a potent spiral until the lavender hued magical power touched the high ceiling.

"Well," Katrina said. "Will you look at that?"

The bubble shrunk with an air sucking, whoosh! Finally, when tiny enough, the magical bubble zoomed into the locket.

The miniature gold heart snapped closed with a click.

"I'm sorry," Claire said while choking on tears. "You must think me weak because I'm crying."

"Of course not," Grace reassured, and patted her gently on the back. "Washington Irving said, 'Tears are not the mark of weakness, but of power. They are messages of overwhelming grief and of unspeakable love.' I happen to agree with him." She finished speaking and gave Claire a gentle hug.

Claire eyed Leeson over Grace's shoulder. His handsome, strong features blurred behind renewed tears. Perhaps the experiences with this new magic opened her heart in ways she never imagined possible.

Certainly Leeson's presence may have meant something different without pondering her parent's love for each other. Their love had touched her on a soulful level.

Never again would she be the same person that had huddled in the bushes at Golden Gate Park.

"That spell work was much easier than I expected," Grace remarked. She eyed Claire's locket. "Leeson, do you think the locket's new magic is potent enough?"

"I'd still like to add our blood," Leeson said while indicating the dagger. "It would connect the four of us. I'd feel better about the stronger magic that a blood binding would induce."

"True," Katrina said. "It would be an easy tweak."

"Wait a sec," Claire said. "What would happen if you add blood?"

The idea of smearing blood on her locket seemed borderline deranged. Especially since love now infused the golden trinket.

Leeson held up the dagger. "This black emerald blade holds great power," he commented while pulling the weapon from the leather sheath. "For one thing, blood would strengthen the magical bond between the four of us."

"How sweet," Katrina teased, "you and I with a bond connection." She twitched her nose in mock amusement.

The muscles in Leeson's face tensed visibly.

"Relax Leeson," Grace urged. "Don't get your feathers in a ruffle."

"This is what we'll do," Grace continued. She moved through the potions book, nimble fingers working in a quick light motion, until a blank page lay open. "Leeson, give me your dagger please."

He flipped the blade away from her and handed Grace the hilt.

"I recall," Grace remarked. "You mentioned the immortal elf Ghillie Dhu created the black emerald blade?"

"Yes," he answered. "It was a gift for my grandmother. The magic infused into the blade eased my journey through the mystical Annwn veil."

Grace pressed the sharp knife point into the book center and cut the blank page loose. A whisper of a sigh escaped as the page parted from its home.

When the parchment was free of the binding, Grace smoothed it on the table. "Katrina, you may donate blood first. The spell requires two blood drops from each of us and one from Claire. Place yours here, please."

Katrina took the knife. "Nice athame."

Leeson grunted, and one side of his mouth twitched, but he did not reply.

Claire tilted her head back and studied his expressive face. "You really don't like each other, do you?"

He shook his head.

"You haven't told her?" Katrina asked with a laugh. "Oh that's rich, Leeson."

"Told me what?"

"There hasn't been time," Leeson replied with a growl.

"What?" Claire insisted.

"That Leeson is a falcon shapeshifter, my dear," Grace remarked. "That's why they don't get along. It's a bird and cat thing."

"You're a falcon?" Claire stepped back, and studied him head to foot. He didn't look any different. The sunlight slanting across his cheeks made him look fierce. Or perhaps that was because he glowered at Katrina as though he wanted her eyes.

"This is not the time," he said, voice edged with sharpness.

"He's right," Grace interjected, putting them back to timely purpose. "Poke your middle finger, Katrina. We're waiting."

Katrina pierced the tender part of her flesh and squeezed two drops of blood side by side onto the parchment. They spread slightly into the texture and formed tiny starbursts.

"I'll go next," Grace remarked, and proceeded with efficient movements. Afterward, she cleaned the blade with a magical wave, and then passed the knife to Leeson. "Put your blood here."

Claire noticed Leeson's blood spots would form a pyramid on the square parchment.

When Leeson finished, Claire released a pent up breath she had been unaware of holding.

Yes, the six blood droplets formed a perfect triangle. Or, depending on a person's perspective, it was a pyramid.

"Now Claire." Grace held the blade forward and gave a reassuring smile. "Please put a drop of your blood in the exact center."

Claire took the athame. Still, she hesitated. Shedding her blood for magic? Somehow, this action seemed as if they were going over top of destiny's head.

"You're sure this is safe?" she asked.

"Absolutely."

The answer came from each of her new friends.

Their affirmative confidence bolstered her belief. That was it. The problem was she had always been a loner. Except for Sister Teresa's frequent influence, she had always made her own choices.

Now, she had new friends.

There was so much unknown about them. The one thing she did know; they were unified in their desire to help.

She pierced the skin of her middle finger, and squeezed one drop of blood into the center of the triangle.

Grace picked up one of her fancy instruments and made quick movements. When finished, Claire saw that Grace had drawn a Celtic symbol using the blood. The intricate lines now formed a protective defense around her single blood drop.

"This will do perfectly," Grace declared while passing a crystal wand over the parchment.

A soft murmur, the parchment shrunk, and then blended into the multi-facetted star on the front of the gold heart.

The magical parchment's presence was completely invisible.

"'Tis the star of truth," Grace explained. "Did you know that?"

"No," Claire answered.

"That's an important element," Grace reassured. "The spell completion is also proof positive of Katrina's necessary presence." She levitated the locket toward Claire. "The star of truth would not have allowed Katrina's blood contribution or participation had her intentions not been pure."

The delicate gold chain rested around Claire's neck with a comforting sensation. She fingered the locket, and then pressed the gold against her chest.

It vanished within the tiny pocket realm.

Katrina pointed to where the necklace had vanished. "Have you ever considered enlarging that little realm?"

"No. Why?" Claire asked.

Katrina returned to her chair and tucked lithe legs beneath her bottom as she sat. Apparently, she was a creature of habit while sitting in repose. "To be invisible, of course."

"Well..." Claire curled a strand of hair behind her ear and glanced at Leeson. "I never considered doing that."

"Perhaps we should," Leeson said. "I hate to admit it, but Katrina may have a point. Are you trained with wand or weapons?"

"Weapons?" she asked, voice crackling. "Why?"

Leeson snorted and waved toward the viewer. "Oh, I don't know. Maybe because there's a Hades daemon after you. One who happens to have legions of bloodthirsty followers?"

"But I've never needed weapons before. If somebody gets too close, I zap them with my hand magic. That's equal to a strong electrical shock."

"Hand magic?" Katrina asked.

Claire palmed some air, wiggled fingers and the magical particles appeared an inch above her hand.

"Cool," Katrina said. "But I agree with Leeson."

"Humph. We can agree on this *one* thing." He plopped across a chair and popped a grape into his mouth.

Katrina twitched her nose at him, and continued, "Your hand magic isn't enough power to fend off legions of daemons if it comes to face to face confrontation. I say we work on the locket magical realm and enlarge the size for you."

"Enlarging the magical realm around your locket could also help with hiding your dreams," Grace explained. "We mustn't forget about that situation. Your dreams still leave you vulnerable to attack from Grismere."

Claire knew that Grace was right. "I just need to slow down a bit. So much new magic is mulling around in my head and confusing all my senses."

"You wouldn't be adding much more," Katrina replied. "The locket realm is already against your skin. Just give the realm permission to become part of you. It'll be super easy. Like this."

Whiskers formed around Katrina's nose. With a sudden move, she leaped from the chair and landed on the table in full black cat persona.

Claire stepped back and nearly landed on Leeson's lap. She scrambled away while wishing heat didn't rush to her cheeks. "But that's different because you're shapeshifting."

Katrina returned to human form and sat on the table edge. "The locket realm is already there, but invisible. If you let the pocket realm surround you, it'll be *shifting* you from visible to invisible."

"We'll need more research first," Grace remarked. "Please don't sit on the table, Katrina. You can start your research in the eastern book-shelves." She motioned toward the book lined wall close to the hallway.

"Leeson," Grace continued. "You should begin with the northern section. Go back several stacks because that section hasn't been updated to our current circumstances."

He nodded, approached the northern wall and pulled a book forward at an angle. The shelf moved to the side. He repeated the process until the fifth bookshelf appeared. That's when he focused intently on finding any information that would help them.

"Claire," Grace remarked. "You may begin with the shelves under the western windows."

"Under?" Claire asked, confused. The windows extended floor to ceiling.

"Here you go," Grace replied, and raised her palm upward. Bookshelves filled to the brim moved up out of the floor until they reached a height of about four feet tall. "Help yourself to anything you choose. I find that if I'm looking for something specific the correct book will show itself."

"Thank you," Claire said, unable to hide an awestruck tone. She walked slowly past the first two sections.

Nothing happened until the third. Two books flew off the shelf. She tucked them under her arm and headed for a soft chair.

"I think I'll leave you to it," Grace declared. "If you need anything, call Miles. He'll give you whatever you require." She exited through the garret doorway with the smooth gracefulness of a soft airwave.

Claire observed her with curiosity and wondered what lay hidden above.

They worked in silence through the afternoon. Each sequestered in their own niche, only the soft sound of pages turning or scratching pens connected their purpose.

Leeson's voice interrupted Claire's quiet mind. *"Knock, knock."*

"Not a joke," Claire replied.

"You said don't enter your mind without an invite."

"Pfft," Claire said. *"You think knocking is an invite?"*

"Got you talking, didn't it?"

"Grrr... What do you want?"

"Just wondered if telepathy still worked after tweaking the locket."

"Apparently it does," Claire replied.

"Should we tell Grace?" He gave no outward appearance they were conversing through mind speak. Instead, he turned the page of his book as if concentrating on the subject written within.

Claire paused and studied the resealed garret doorway. *"No."*

"She already knows," Katrina said while curling up in her chair and opening another book on her lap.

Leeson scowled at her from across the room. "How'd you do that? Intrude."

"Seems I can hear and sense your telepathy. Grace can, too. I can't mind speak though."

"That doesn't make sense," Claire said.

Katrina shrugged without looking from her book. "Magical gifts come as they are. It's always best to accept and move forward into utilizing them the best way possible. Why fret when you receive a present?"

"Doesn't that depend on the gift?" Claire asked. "After all, some magical gifts are a challenge to work through."

"Nothing is given to you that you cannot handle," Katrina said, repurposing wisdom.

"I've always thought that bit of wisdom was off kilter. Circumstances vary."

"Of course they do," Katrina remarked. "That's where life contrast comes from. You wouldn't want to be bored." She paused. "Speaking of handling gifts," Katrina continued, while slipping her legs from beneath her and sitting straighter. "I've found something."

Claire leaned over the back of Katrina's chair so she could see. "Pocket realm?"

"It's perfect. Essentially, that's what you created for the locket. We'll just make one big enough for you."

Claire fingered her hair and twisted a curl. "I still think I should stay with you and Leeson."

| Part Three |
Golden Star of Truth

There is nothing in life to be feared.
It is only to be understood.
Madam Currie

* * * * * * * * *

[4] Witch in a Bubble

Their first attempt at creating a pocket realm for Claire failed. Her feet kept showing. The realm also tickled so much Claire couldn't stop giggling.

"This borders on insane," Claire sputtered inside the second bubble. In her mind that's what they were making. *A witch in a bubble. Ha ha.*

Even with the giggling, air inside was in short supply and her lungs rebelled. A band tightened around her ribcage and squeezed. That put a halt to humor as she struggled to breathe.

Possible suffocation was not her idea of fun. She threw tingling arms outward in an unplanned and brash movement.

The magic from her hands sprayed across the room. Havoc exploded. Books crashed off shelves. A large porcelain vase shattered.

"I'm sorry," Claire gasped and coughed. "I couldn't breathe. Felt closed in." She inhaled deeply and released slowly. The action soothed the edges of her agitation. "It must have been a natural response to panic about smothering."

Katrina waved a pretty, beribboned pink wand above the broken vase. The pieces danced together and fused into a repaired vase. "No loss. That's a strong projection power you have."

"You were afraid?" Leeson asked. "Why?"

"Not being able to breathe?" Claire retorted. "Who wouldn't fear that?"

"But we're right here," Leeson said. "If the magic doesn't work, the three of us functioning together will get you out."

"Hold on a sec," Katrina said. She flipped through the thick pages of an oversized, leather bound book. "I saw something about this."

"About this?" Claire asked, completely flustered by the thought that her experience could be written within an ancient tome.

"Yes. Here it is," Katrina answered. "I didn't put the two together."

"What are you referring to?" Leeson asked.

"Emotions and power," Katrina said. She cleared her throat and started reading. "Be aware. The magic of a pocket realm holds emotions. Use extreme caution. Heightened feelings will magnify tenfold. Understanding the situation will improve your results."

"Whoa. Back up," Claire said. "Since I couldn't breathe inside, the magic of this bubble thingy caused me to freak out because it holds my emotions? Then the bubble *multiplied* my heightened feelings?"

"It's like you're in a jar." Katrina made motions with her hands, including screwing a lid on top.

Claire grimaced.

"Everyone projects their emotions," Katrina continued with her explanation. "Even someone who doesn't have magic. It's like being in a room with a grumpy person and suddenly you're grumpy. You catch the projection of their bad mood."

Claire gnawed her bottom lip. "Project emotion? You mean when I shoved away and all these books flew off the shelves?"

"Yes." Leeson took the leather tome from Katrina and scanned the page. "It's interesting, the statement here on page three hundred ninety-five about understanding the situation."

"Oh, I understand," Claire growled. "This'll never work. I still think staying with you is better."

"You don't have battle training," Leeson insisted while handing the tome back to Katrina. "I refuse to allow you in the fighting zone."

"That's absurd!" If she was supposed to be aware of her emotions, now would have been a good time for Weyer to attack. She could have flayed him. "Didn't I just knock books off the shelves?"

He moved fast. Suddenly nose to nose with her, Leeson vibrated with stubborn insistence. "But you can't control your projection magic and there isn't time to master the power. As for this 'bubble thingy', you so eloquently call it, this magic isn't much different from when we were in the San Andreas Fault tunnel. You remember your reaction to falling into the pit?"

She nodded.

"Then focus," he insisted. "Channel your emotions into your magic. Take advantage of them instead of fearing their result. Engage the pocket realm...*now*."

With a ferocious growl, she snapped hands over top her head.

A bubble formed around her. Imperfect at best, the iridescent magic contained Swiss cheese holes everywhere.

"Face your fear," Leeson said.

"I'm not afraid! I am furious with you!"

"Anger has the same effect as fear. Do it! Channel the emotions into plugging those holes."

She closed eyes tight and allowed the anger to build under her ribcage. Rubbing her fingertips together assisted the process.

"Perfect!" Katrina said. "Now think invisible."

She opened her eyes, stuck her tongue out at Leeson. *You can't see me!*

"Not bad," he said, and gazed at the spot where she stood. "I can still see your toes, but you aren't giggling like a silly schoolgirl."

"Argh!" she roared and shoved toward his head.

A stiff breeze tossed his hair, but made him grin.

The wall behind him opened and Grace stepped through the doorway from the garret. "I think that's my cue to return."

Shock pierced Claire's brain. With a gasp, she dissolved the bubble and stared.

"Do I look all right?" Grace asked, and then twirled, showing off her magical glamour. Claire's own face smiled back at her.

"Um... yes," Clare whispered. "You look exactly like me."

[5] *Elemental Gateway*

Leeson gazed through the elegant black wrought iron gate. Even without the assistance of falcon vision he saw everything clearly. The moon, round in the fullest sense, brightened the night sky and illuminated the expansive estate grounds.

The concrete drive reflected lunar brilliance and curved around a center fountain.

Frankly, he wondered why such a renowned wizard would have concrete anywhere near his home because the manufactured feature intruded upon the earth's magical effectiveness.

Water in the fountain spouted six feet into the air and tumbled into a large stone base. The heavy noise, like waves crashing a rocky shore, carried upon the air and intruded upon any potential peace and tranquility.

Behind the surging water, a white limestone Mediterranean styled mansion dominated the landscape. The stones of the massive home held a luminescent finish and matched the brilliant moon in perfection.

Moments passed while he studied everything with an eye toward strategy. "This is where you want to battle Weyer?"

He spun his gaze downward and studied Grace's face. It was odd, seeing her with a glamour that presented Claire's face to observers. "What makes you think this will work?"

"It's perfect," Grace replied. "We will have home advantage."

He grunted. "Except this isn't home and we aren't familiar with the layout."

"That shouldn't be a problem," Grace commented while quirking a silver darkened brow. "You're a quick study."

Katrina moved from the shadows and pressed her face against the bars. "Claire is safely tucked away. We'd best get started. It'll be midnight soon."

"Let me guess," Leeson growled. "At the strike of witching hour you turn into a black cat."

"I have an appointment."

"Excuse me?" Leeson asked. "In the middle of preparations? This is probably one of the biggest battles of our life. I knew you couldn't be trusted!"

"First," Katrina replied in a husky purr. "I've seven more lives to go. Second, I'm meeting Abraham. He'll be able to help."

Grace stepped between them and passed painted fingers over the lock. The mechanism snapped, and the gate swung open. "Bicker later. Let's get started."

[6] *Wicked*

One thing for sure, Claire still didn't feel comfortable.

This bubble, pocket realm, in-between space, or whatever anyone called it, magnified emotions and all five senses.

She paced across the concrete floor while her magic popped and snapped.

Debris from past occupants littered the basement room and added to a sickly musty odor.

Yes, the smell affected the way she experienced the magical bubble. The interior surface of the bubble pushed everything back into her skin. She pressed her lips together in an attempt to shut out the rancid, greasy taste from the stench of old French fries.

Mingled odors and the atmosphere created from magical blending within the bubble heightened her five senses beyond anything she had ever experienced.

She paused in her pacing to adjust and monitor her emotions.

According to the book Katrina had been studying, understanding and acknowledging what happened during this metaphysical experience would ease the process. So she closed eyes and tried to envision pleasant things.

Images of playful puppies, kittens and chocolate ice cream coursed through her thoughts. A rainbow she saw in her youth flashed through her mind with colorful rays and that hopeful vision led to some favorite songs.

At last, she breathed evenly, and hummed a few bars of an old song.

Although she had reestablished good feelings

and calmed the bubble interior to almost bearable, she still experienced a shiver along her spine.

Outside her pocket realm, the room was cold due to the concrete floor and refrigerated air pumping through an ancient venting system.

The song in her mind stopped. She studied a discarded fast food sack. A mouse scurried out of the interior and raced to a crack in an old crate. The tail tip vanished.

Hiding like me.

In Claire's mind, this plan failed to be comfortable, and gave a deep resonance of dark omen which implied coming disaster.

True, the pocket formed a perfect bubble around her, but she didn't believe the untested magic was impenetrable.

Claire tried not to think about Katrina's insistence that she disappear within this bubble. She had created this magic to protect the gold locket, not herself.

As for Leeson, he had been stubborn as a rock in his argument.

Now, away from them and hiding within this pocket realm, the memory of his insistence burned across her mind. *"Don't carry a weapon unless you know what it's like to have that weapon turned on you."*

His assertion that she hide because of no training made her angry. *Some master plan! Ugh!*

"Piffle butt!" she roared.

For once saying those words didn't make her feel better. She sighed and leaned against the wall.

That was one good thing. She could still experience the environment of this dreary basement. The good side of that awareness was that she would also know instantly when Leeson and Katrina returned.

She reached for a particle of hope that soon she would be safe.

Those moments in Golden Gate Park were behind her now. She was grateful for new friends.

These new magical experiences moved like a rushing river, but she understood their importance toward a brighter future.

The heavy steel security door across the room creaked upon rusty hinges as it opened.

A weird looking man stepped over the threshold. His skin hung on such a bony structure that Claire envisioned him as a horror movie scarecrow.

Wispy hair, greased to disgustingness, spread across narrow, scrunched shoulders. A matching beard lay on his chest like death.

Gold teeth, braided into the beard like trophies of war, adorned this man with a wicked legacy. There was an odd device on top of his head.

She cringed and pressed against the wall. *He can't see me.*

Mister no name scanned the room with deliberate, unhurried fascination.

Claire held her breath. She could not slow her heart beat. It pounded under her breasts and reverberated in her ears.

A low laugh emerged from the scarecrow stalker. "Sweet Lucifer," he said. His voice crackled on the air and penetrated her pocket realm. "I believe there's a tasty treat hiding here."

In fast mind speak, Claire reached out to Leeson.

Leeson are you there?

Silence.

Who knew the brain could be so quiet? Panic

stirred under her skin and gained momentum with each passing second. *It's just the heightened emotions in a bubble thing.*

Claire didn't want to feel helpless. That was because she really didn't think of herself as wimpy.

Just that right now everything in her life sped by on fast forward.

New magic always took awhile to get used to. At this point, there had been no extra practice to learn the smaller details.

Since having legions of daemons after her made Claire feel alone, she tuned into her new friends and their magical link through the locket.

Was Leeson too far away for their mind connection to work?

Leeson!

The scarecrow's bony fingers reached upward in malicious intent.

Claire cringed at the sight of nasty fingernails.

Scarecrow twiddled with the odd object on the top of his head, and then pulled it forward and down.

Pilot goggles? Huh?

Mind speaking resulted in absolute quiet and multiplied her kaleidoscopic emotions. Goose bumps spread up her arms, bringing a spine deep shiver of wicked cold along with more tense moments.

"Let's see what we have here," nasty scarecrow said. He slid the blue lenses that were framed by muddy grey goggles down over jaundiced eyes.

She already knew the answer.

He froze and stared at her in the hidden pocket realm.

She was no longer invisible.

He cackled.

It was the scratchiest sound she had ever heard. The frequency of his wickedness vibrated along her skin with a sinful portent.

"You..." Somehow, she lost her voice and breath. *Must be his magic?*

She pressed against the cinder block wall and forced in a deep breath. The action took strong will, but blended her magic through fingers and feet.

Exhaling pushed her pulse into the porous brick, and then the stony earth.

Scarecrow stepped forward, shortening the distance between them.

The door slammed closed behind him with a *bang!*

The wicked face split into a leering grin. He withdrew a curved bladed knife from the tattered coat interior.

With devious teasing, he flicked the blade. The deadly visual effect needed no spoken words.

Focused breathing intensified the earth energies coming through her hands and feet and nourished her magic. She found her voice. "You can't touch me."

"Ya fae are all alike," he said with a sneer. The lines on his face angled into the goggles and created a fearsome aberration.

His speech was odd. Each time he spoke the letter 'a' sound caught on his tongue and hung in the air like a wicked pinch.

"Ya think," he drawled while still flicking the knife, "da earth energies protect ya. Stupid witch bitch."

He approached while the knife spun playfully between nasty fingers. The blade was sparkling clean compared to his hands.

She refused to move. If she believed, then her

pocket realm would protect. Claire stiffened her resolve.

She would go down fighting, weapon training be damned.

"Yes, I'm a witch. Fae too. As for bitch... Anyone that tells me I'm a Beautiful, Intelligent, Thoughtful Caring Human is flirting. You are not my type. So shove off."

He stood within a foot of her boundary. "Smart mouth, eh? Word on da street there's a reward fer snatchin' ya."

The bony head tilted, and he eyed her top to bottom. "Don't see da value. Weyer wants ya dead by 'is own hand. Didn't say what condition ya need ta be thou. Ya tongue'll be the last thing I cut. Wanna hear ya screams furst."

He licked his lips with a quick flick of a pointed tongue.

Hands at her side, Claire curled fingers so her magic would build in velocity. "You're crazy if you think kidnapping me will get you what you want. It'll get you dead."

He cackled and poked the barrier with his knife.

The initial contact between blade and bubble melded and transferred sensation to her skin.

Pain of the bubble piercing rippled along her arm. Sudden realization sharpened her emotions even deeper. The bubble was a second skin and could cause direct injury if damaged.

Claire clenched her teeth and continued rubbing fingertips against thumbs. Magic flowing through heightened emotions filled her with an awesome sensation of floating. She relished the joy of that emotion and allowed the bubble to multiply and feed her magic.

The knife penetrated the bubble surface.

Blood trickled down her forearm.

The knife action was slow, but from her angle appeared like something being pushed through Jell-O. She decided not to stand still and let this monster touch her on a physical level.

Claire moved quick and to the left.

He growled at the evasive maneuver, pushed the knife faster and succeeded in making a large hole.

She ignored the pain of injury and pulsed magic through her fingers. *Intention guides magic.*

Without hesitating, he climbed through his cut window.

The moment his foot touched the floor, she impacted the bottom of her boot heel with the outside of his knee.

With a straggle toothed roar, he toppled to the floor, arms flailing the air in surprised reaction.

The knife bounced and skidded away.

Claire ran toward the grey steel door. She wasn't sure what would happen since they were in the bubble together.

There was a rending tear as though an earthquake hit the room.

Scarecrow roared in pain, but managed to get to his knees. On all fours, he scrambled for the knife.

Damn, should've gotten the knife. No time.

Leeson's mind speak absence fed a persistent urgency to escape this newest threat to her safety. They should have checked the effectiveness of longer distances before implementing their plan.

She rushed toward the door.

Scarecrow tackled her from behind.

In an intense scramble, she flipped onto her

back and wiggled like a maddened fiend.

Dirty hands touched her skin, but could not hold on. Blood from the arm injury smeared and made her arm slippery. She pushed palms upward and connected with his nasty face.

Zap!

"AHH!" he roared in painful desperation.

Singed beard became the dominate odor and pillowed around them with pungent vileness. The daemon convulsed with electrical energy. The echo of his painful holler beat her into renewed action.

Claire rolled away and got to her feet. Breathing hard, this time she made it to the door. With her uninjured arm, she reached for the knob.

"Tricky," the scarecrow said with a cackle. He grabbed her and wrenched her around to face him.

Stunned, he had recovered so quickly, she raised a hand to fend him off again.

"Won't work," he said and tightened grubby fingers around her wrist. "Ya just shared yer power."

She opened her mouth, but no sound came out.

In slow motion, nasty fingers moved in wicked anticipation, he touched her cheek with a gleeful laugh.

Electricity surged through Claire's skin. Every molecule in her body crumpled.

The sensation of falling proved the most surreal experience in her life to date. She shook with electrical shock at the same time she froze stiff.

Nothing numbed the pain. She screamed inside her head when the cold stone floor met her cheek.

Conscious, but unable to move, she could do nothing.

Scarecrow picked her up, and flung her over

his shoulder.

Piffle butt, Leeson! Where are you?

Normal feeling gradually eased over her body. She breathed deeply even though the action filled her nostrils with rancid scarecrow eau de cologne.

He stomped up the steps and walked through the outer door with a rolling gait. In the narrow alley he turned left.

Draped over his shoulder, Claire had an upside down view of his back. She noticed a slit in the side seam of his long grungy coat.

The hilt of another knife peeked out when he repositioned her for a better grip.

Fully recovered from being zapped, she wiggled and kicked while trying to reach the concealed knife. Zapping him wouldn't do any good now that he had stolen her power. She needed another plan.

"Be still." His broad hand smacked her on the bottom.

Clare went limp. *Must be his magic. Wonder where he stole that power from?*

Leeson? No answer. Well she had to try. Her nose itched because of the smell. She tried to twitch her nose. *Katrina.* Why hadn't she thought of her before?

Katrina can you hear me?

Everything shifted as scarecrow flung her forward.

She collided with something unknown. The grotesque sound of her body thumping against an unseen landing place made her wince.

Pain followed and traced along the nerve endings under her skin. Claire groaned.

She was no longer over his shoulder. The tossing movement happened so fast that a fog of confusion rattled in her brain. She tried feeling the container he had dropped her into by sending hands exploring.

"Stop that," he snarled. He grabbed her wrists, and before she knew what he had done, rope circled and tightened against sensitive skin.

She shook her head trying to clear the fog. *Must be his weird magic... Can't think.*

Smack!

Stars burst behind her eyes.

"Be still!" He slammed the top down.

Darkness swallowed her.

[7] Elemental

Leeson, Grace and Katrina stepped through the estate gateway and approached the water fountain with deeply ingrained caution, always on the alert for any threat.

Even though Grace knew the owners weren't home, there was always the possibility the hound pack had already tracked them.

"Let's change this up a bit," Grace remarked, and paused next to the circular fountain. She raised hands and smoothed the air above the basin of water. Then she clapped gently and wiggled fingers in a floating downward motion. The water shifted and began falling in gentle droplets as though a sweet summer rain.

"Oh yes," Katrina said. She pulled her pink wand from a back pocket in her black jeans. Making dotting motions, she introduced fuchsia colored flowers to float on the wet surface.

"Can't believe," Leeson retorted, "you carry such a sissy wand."

"Pink is my favorite color." She tossed her head, tucked the wand back into her pocket and sashayed toward the front door. Her black cat tail morphed out and swung in perfect rhythm with her steps. "Besides," she said over her shoulder, "you should know, the simple fact of emotional attachment adds potency to my wand work."

He rolled his eyes at her blatant cattiness.

"Simple magic always carries more weight in spell work," Grace interjected while she searched through her jacket pockets.

"Lose something?" he asked.

"Can't find the key," Grace remarked.

"You opened the front gate with magic." He reached toward the ornate brass door latch. "Do the same here."

Katrina stopped him.

"Can't," Grace replied. "Ah, here's the key." She pulled her hand out of a deep pocket and showed them the large brass and stone key. It was intricately carved and completely filled her small hand. Grace inserted the shaped stone end into the lock and held the brass while she turned.

Unlike usual locks, apparently there was an odd trick to this one.

After one turn, Grace tapped the end of the key with an index finger, waited, and then reversed the action. The lock clicked.

"Charles has a special alarm system," Grace remarked. "In this case, using magic would have set sirens blaring. The key is completely necessary. We wouldn't want the kind of police he has protecting this place to arrive and stop our plans."

Leeson stepped over the threshold. "Thought he gave us permission to be here."

"Of course he did," Grace remarked. "How do you suppose I got the key code?"

He whistled. The oval entrance hall boasted a double stairway that followed curved walls to a height of three stories.

Gold gilded marble columns supported the staircases and ceiling in majestic splendor.

Midway up the stairs, two oversized painted landscapes hung in ornate frames, and gave an impression of otherly worlds within the traditional architecture of the home.

The marble floor beneath them bore an intricate circle design in the center of the oversized room.

The space was gargantuan, and he had to admit, perfect for their purpose.

All this opulence he took in while spinning on his boot heel. "Plenty of necessary elements," he said, and waved toward the stairs on his left. "Height increases air flow. The stair rails are metal, and the column caps are plated with gold."

"Personally," Katrina said as she traced the veins in a marble column. "I like this. It's perfect in attitude and action."

Pink polished fingernails exposed, she caressed the marble while purring. Her tail wrapped the column as she snuggled and slinked around the cool marble.

"You're perverted," Leeson growled.

"Rrr..." she said, and winked. "I can hardly wait to see what's revealed from these lines. No two are alike, you know. Marble veins are the perfect metamorphism for my purpose. You'll see."

He turned away with a head shake and searched for Grace. Katrina's proclivities to cat behavior always annoyed him. She knew it, and performed with purposeful actions that resulted in exasperating his falcon senses. The best defense was to ignore feline behavior.

He discovered Grace poking around the furniture. "Please don't tell me you're about to get fresh with that sofa."

Grace laughed. "Just checking the wood quality. Thank goodness Charles has these pieces. The chairs are mahogany. That includes those in the dining room. These will serve my purpose."

"Place is rather sparse, if you ask me. Considering it's a nineteen million dollar home, your friend Charles doesn't seem to own many luxuries."

"When he's here, Charles lives in quarters upstairs. I assure you he has plenty to keep himself comfortable. Besides, you of all people should know that what one sees is not always the full picture."

"For example," she replied, and walked into the dining room. "Take these mahogany chairs as a magical element. Trees have a natural synergy with air. That means these chairs contain that same phenomenon of connectivity. Blended in the same room with the crystal chandelier, which is also an earth gift, we can magnify our magical power."

Her matter of fact tone gave him a burst of sudden insight. "That's why you have such an extensive library. I mean, aside from your love of reading. Each page is a link to a magical element. All those connections eventually draw back to air— your most potent element."

He touched the surface of an ornate sideboard. "Never considered any of that before."

"You're young," Grace remarked. "Think we'll insert some live trees for added measure." She pointed her crystal wand at the marble floor, made a spiral and then drew straight toward the ceiling. A tree sprouted and grew tall enough to brush gently against the ceiling.

Happy with the results, Grace repeated the process and planted more trees around the dining room.

With each new planting the air moved in a gentle breeze. Whispering leaves filled him with a deep avian restlessness.

To shake the effect off, he approached the western wall. Large windows actually turned out to be floor to ceiling glass sliding doors. He pushed them open until the entire western wall of the room became an extension to the outside patio.

"Interesting," Katrina said as she sauntered through the dining room eyeing the new trees, and then exited through the open window. "Although I bet it's not quite as much fun as twelve marble columns primed and ready for battle."

Leeson stood next to an empty fire pit. "Blagh. Sorry to have missed that."

"Funny," she said with a habitual twitch of her nose. "You're a complete failure at sarcasm."

"No. You just don't get me."

"Oh, I understand you perfectly." She twitched her tail, took hold of the end and caressed. "Where's Grace? It's almost midnight and I wanted to say bye before I leave."

He glanced around the dining room. "She was just here." There was no sign of Grace. He strode across the room and reentered the large entrance hall.

Strong evidence of Grace being there changed the previous appearance of the room. Now, several trees grew where none had been before. Grapevines climbed the banister and scented magical flowers lined the circular design in the center of the floor.

However, there was no Grace.

"Look!" Katrina said, and pointed toward the framed landscape that hung over the staircase to their right. The portrait Katrina indicated was a colorful depiction of a seaside beach cottage.

He saw a light move within the gilded frame. Startled by the odd occurrence, he took the steps two at a time until he stood close to the portrait.

"Well bugger," he remarked. "Never saw one of these before, have you?"

Katrina stared at the portrait. "No."

He hesitated, unsure whether to touch or not. "Do you suppose Grace got sucked in or went in on her own?"

"I've never known Grace to get sucked into anything."

"Truth is, neither have I," he answered. First, he glanced down the stairs.

No sign of Grace.

He cocked his head, set his jaw and then stuck his head through the canvas. Once past the initial shock of getting through the semi-stiff surface he saw Grace.

"What are you doing?" he asked as he stepped into the extra world of portraiture magic.

Katrina followed close on his heels.

"Isn't this fascinating," Grace commented breathlessly. "I must get one."

"A virtual world?" Leeson glanced around at the quaint cottage tucked amidst rocks and sand. "Looks like a vacation home. Ocean's not bad if you're into low hanging, dark clouds and eerie atmosphere."

"It's where Charles comes to write," Grace explained. "That old goat. I'm going to scold him for not sharing."

"Um, Grace?" Katrina said while tucking her tail behind her. It vanished. "Ever think there might be a good reason he didn't share?" She pointed to a large boulder.

A cold wind smacked Leeson on the back of his neck and sped down his spine. He also noticed Katrina's cat attitude had shifted to one of extreme caution. "Bloody hell!" he shouted, grabbed Grace and ran for the portrait canvas.

From this side of the canvas, the interior of the mansion and stairs hung in the air like a nighttime moon, and looked just as far away.

Grace protested. "Leeson, what's wrong?"

"The rocks aren't real!" Katrina shouted.

A nearby boulder melted into a rushing wave of crimson water from the River Styx. The magical torrent chased them with a hellish tsunami roar upon a nasty sulfuric wind.

Feet pounding on wet sand and rough rocks, they ran.

Since Grace couldn't fly, earthbound magic held them to the ground. With each step they took, the glamour Grace wore to fool Weyer slipped and melted a little, revealing her true identity.

The loss of magic involved in the glamour spell also weakened Grace, and she stumbled over her own feet.

Katrina grabbed Grace's arm and helped her over moving stones that had sprouted crab like feet. The skittering movement was meant to trip them. "Damn!" Katrina growled and urged Grace forward.

Finally at the portrait, Grace tripped again, and then gripped the ornate frame while gasping for air.

"Can't stop now!" Leeson roared, trying to be heard over the red wall of River Styx water rushing toward them.

He picked Grace up and they burst through the canvas breathless.

The cursed water pushed after them.

Leeson put Grace on a stair and swung his hand toward the canvas portal.

The portrait closed with a slurping sound. Tense, he leaned against the banister and struggled to get his breath.

From the other side of the canvas wickedness lashed in fury against the barrier. The hellion wrath echoed in the entrance hall.

"Did any of the water get on you?" he asked Grace and Katrina.

"No," they answered in unison.

Several crimson splashes had landed on the steps and slithered into the corner.

"That can't be good." Grace pulled her crystal wand from a hiding place within her clothing and moved it in a spiral over the wet spots. They vanished.

"Oh no," Leeson groaned while staring at the open front door.

"I wondered what had happened to you, Katrina," a man said. He stood just inside the threshold while letting in the morning sunshine.

"It's daytime." Leeson remarked. Shock rattled him with a dark omen of impending doom. *"Claire!"*

Silence.

"What happened?" he shouted at the man, assuming him to be Charles, the mansion owner.

The man's eyes grew round. "I have no idea. I came searching for Katrina. She missed our appointment last night. Very unlike her..."

"The portrait," Katrina interrupted. "It must be a time portal."

"Oh dear," Grace remarked in a disquieting tone, and pulled at the duplicate of a blouse Claire had worn. Now that her glamour magic was gone, nothing fit properly. A quick wave of Grace's wand and one of her own airy blue dresses appeared.

"Precisely," Leeson growled. "I'm going to get Claire!"

Grace touched his arm. "Leeson wait."

Heart racing, he forced himself to stand in one place.

Strands of hair hung free of Grace's French braid, but her expression was still calm. "I know you're worried. Let Katrina go. You and I need to discuss this development with Abraham and Charles. I'm sure Charles didn't know his sanctuary had been invaded by a Hades water daemon."

"There's a daemon at Charles' cottage?" Abraham started up the stairs. Once in front of the portrait, he gazed intently into the image. "I don't see anything amiss."

"We're wasting time," Leeson argued. "I need to go."

"Leeson," Katrina said. "I'll get Claire. You stay here and work with Grace and Abraham."

Leeson shook Grace from his arm, and moved toward the door.

"They'll need your flight," Katrina insisted. "I swear I'll bring her back safely."

He paused and stared at the sunshine streaming in through the open door. "There's something wrong. I just know. I told her she would be safe."

Katrina stepped between him and the door. "I'll bring her home. I promise."

[8] Illusions

Claire's awareness returned in gradual increments. The first thing that shook her awake was the smell. The odor of moldy rope and the coppery scent of blood mingled with her own sweat. The combined scents burned her sinuses.

She didn't open her eyes. Reading the magical essence of her location was important, and required her other four senses. But not sight.

All ten fingers ached bone deep. She tried moving them and groaned when pain shot from fingertips to her palms. The ache could happen if she overused her magic. She must have been fighting something during the spell induced sleep.

Claire's wrists itched where the rope bound them together. With intense wiggling she managed to thumb the locket. Apparently, the scarecrow had not seen her treasure. *Good.*

The stiffness in her body from lying curled on her side in a box made her muscles ache. It was a tight fit because the box had an oblong shape.

Skinny as she was, she squeezed in by pressing her shins tightly against the interior. She moved her spine and winced when the vertebra cracked.

The box was long enough to straighten her legs. She did, in slow motion.

Eyes still closed, Claire encouraged her aura to pulse within close quarters. She relaxed into the vibration of life force and realized the box was an unlined coffin.

Claire had been in a coffin before. Last year, at Hallo-scare in Akron, when she worked as a corpse and zombie she had been the only female willing to climb inside a death box.

She grunted, and then winced when the sound bounced back and scrambled along her skin.

Shudders moved all the way to her toes. The resonance from her groan was creepy.

After her initial reaction, Claire noticed a soft hissing sound.

Air. Fresh and coming in somehow. The oxygen helped clear her thoughts. She rubbed thumbs against the locket.

Leeson?

Silence.

But the heart locket warmed. That was a good sign. Communication with Leeson was cut off, but the golden magic still worked.

She opened her eyes. Pitch blackness engulfed and surrounded every inch of her aching body. Darkness didn't frighten her. Instead, it aided her thoughts.

Scarecrow would eventually open her prison.

Be ready, she thought and took a breath.

Yes, the fresh air was coming in through a tube. The villain had probably used the same system to drug her, but now wanted her awake. That meant he was getting ready and would make his move soon.

Well, she could do that, too.

Earlier, when she had been in the bubble, emotions had been all over the place. Maybe with practice she would eventually be able to use that form of protection.

She had experienced an epiphany while they worked the locket spell. Using the new idea became her next goal.

Time to get started. First, these smelly ropes.

Claire focused on the exact moment she realized a unified connection with her dead parents. That had happened during the locket spell amidst a river of flowing tears.

The tear element wasn't necessary now because the memory of their release was a potent experience at the core of her being.

Her parents had always been with her, but she had been unaware of their presence.

But now, awareness fed magic—the most primal magic of all—parental love for their child.

She knew that now.

Okay mom, she thought with an exhale. *These ropes are a nuisance.*

With the locket between chilled fingers, she pushed a vision of freed hands into reality.

The ropes softened, began to dissolve, and then in a breath of soft lighted faery glimmer, the bindings vanished.

Blood rushed into fingertips and returned warmth with a tingling surge of magical life force.

She rested for a moment while encouraging her mind to relax. It was part of a system Sister Teresa had taught.

If someone realized the simple but powerful gift of God's breath they could use its magic for healing. It was a valuable lesson from Sister Teresa and Claire used it now.

The action of inhale was appreciation for precious life.

Relax.

Exhale with an intoned *thank you* and it magnified the potency. The body was a temple and always listened when spoken to with respect.

She had used this system frequently and it always worked, unless she was in a funky bubble.

The fresh, clean air coming into the coffin tube nourished and strengthened.

Pain energy shot downward and out the bottom of her left foot. Intense as the throbbing was, she bit back a yell.

Exhale...that's happened before. Pain out. Relax.

Relief was successful because now the cut on her arm didn't hurt.

She passed fingers over the injury made when scarecrow pierced the bubble and therefore her skin. The cut had healed partially. The ridge of a scab appeared under her fingertips, and no pain encouraged the plan forward.

Maybe this'll work.

"Thank you," she said, low voiced, but confident. Even appreciation had magical potency, and she knew those two words empowered.

"Now," she whispered, "to fool the scarecrow." Claire pressed on the locket. The gold totem vanished into its protective realm. Ever present and powerful, the heart centered magic would sustain her through the coming crisis.

To insure a perfect illusion, she placed palms together as though in prayer. "By the power of three times three, give scarecrow exactly what he expects to see."

The coffin vibrated with the sounds of locks being opened. The top swung upward.

"Looky, look. Princess is awake," the scarecrow said, and cackled with wicked, demented pleasure.

Claire blinked, and raised hands to shield eyes. Although the bare bulb hanging from the ceiling wasn't bright, the naked light still made the room lighter than the blackness inside the coffin.

She stalled his plans by rubbing her eyes and taking longer than necessary to grow accustomed to the brighter surroundings.

Dry lips became another stalling tool as she

licked them, and then gradually lowered fingers to see scarecrow leering. "Told you," she said huskily through a dry throat. "Shove off. You're not my type."

Within her mind, Claire held the focus of injuries so he would see her as she had been when he stuffed her into the coffin. She faked a groan.

"Poor girly," he said with a wicked guffaw. "Don't worry; we've time ta play b'fore Grismere gets here."

Wait for it.

Bony fingers grasped her upper arm and pulled her to sit.

She flinched away, pretending his action hurt. Under lowered lashes, she studied the room while still keeping the illusion of tied hands pressed together.

A large black cauldron, its contents boiling and emitting occasional popping sounds took up one half side of an ancient stove. Steam hovered in the air. Claire put hands over her nose in an attempt to avoid the smell.

There was a sink with a short countertop which extended to a rickety pile of old wooden crates stacked in the corner. Wherever this place was, it certainly lacked a homey touch.

"Outta the box." Scarecrow grabbed her arm and yanked.

For a scrawny man, he was strong. He jerked until she was half out of the coffin and released her in midair.

Claire toppled to the floor.

He cackled and kicked.

It hurt, but she had been kicked harder before, so she cursed under her breath and tried to clutch her middle.

It's all a show.

On her way down to the floor, Claire saw the goggles. If her plan was to work, they needed to disappear.

Scarecrow had tossed them on the table, probably thought she couldn't get to them.

The locket warmed against her skin inside the secret hiding place.

The floor chilled her forehead as she frowned at the floorboards.

A man's voice spoke upon the air. "There's something greater than anger, vanquishes fear and obliterates hatred."

The man's voice was one she thought she recognized. It was her father, Alexander Brinawell.

"I remember," Claire whispered, pressed her cheek against her forearm and wondered how long she should maintain the magical glamour of injury and physical weakness.

Scarecrow bent, grabbed her hair and yanked.

The yell that burst forth was not faked.

"Our love," Claire's mother spoke inside her head, "united Alex and me. Joining made us one. You are an extension of our love. Know that, and acknowledge the powerful connection in your heart. We are always with you."

The scarecrow tossed her about as if she were lightweight as a rag doll.

She banged against the coffin and leaned there for a moment. Pain radiated from a new bruise on her arm and the movement had twisted her left knee.

Rough contact with the coffin edge split her jeans and skin. She tried to put weight on the knee and winced, but stood stubbornly.

Warmth blossomed from the locket. In Claire's

mind, the warmth mirrored the exact shape of the diamond centered star of truth engraved in the heart shaped gold.

She sucked her lower lip in and inhaled. The action of pulling the breath inward made the heat of the locket seep deeper into her skin. She dipped her face, hid a soft smile, and mimicked injury with a whimper.

Sure she hurt, but if the daemon thought she was worse than the injuries actually were, she would have the advantage.

Claire focused her thoughts, centering with pinpoint focus on her injured knee. She sent just enough magic to dull the ache because it was important to reserve strength for battle. Then she shifted her shoulders as if shaking off pain and whimpered again.

Excited by her misery, scarecrow laughed and reached for her bound hands.

She responded with a fast kick at his legs.

He roared in fury.

Claire tucked her head, flipped in an old gymnastics move and scrambled away by shoving against the wall with her foot. Since one knee was still injured, she used the other, and then decided to land on her hands. That meant separating them.

Now, he knew the ropes that appeared to bind her had been an illusion.

Wide eyed shock passed over his bony features and his beard bristled in electrical anger as if wind tossed it. He roared, "Trickery won't save you! Fae magic will kill you!"

"We'll see," she hissed and leapt onto the table. The goggles, cold between her fingers, gave Claire a sense of accomplishment. She clasped them to her stomach, rolled off the table and slid between crooked table legs.

Now, breathing hard and sheltered by the tabletop, she pulled the goggle strap down over her head and let them hang around her neck.

Scarecrow, knife in hand, stuck his head under the table.

Hot steam escaped from the black cauldron on the ancient stove. Claire could see her former prison, the coffin behind him. She crab crawled, putting distance between her and his nasty face. Once at a safe distance, she winced, placed a palm on the knee and gave it another mini burst of low level healing.

"There's nowhere to run," he snarled, and the lines on his face moved with eerie malice.

Claire tilted her head and resisted the renewed spark of anxiety that sputtered under her ribcage. There was something strange about the knee. A creepy crawly sensation under the skin worried her, but she shoved the injury out of her mind.

This was it. She had to escape and get back to Leeson and Katrina.

Claire said the first thing that came to her mind. "Happy birthday." Then she pushed out of the table shelter and landed on the nasty daemon.

Hands and feet flailed as each fought to gain the dominate position.

Pain pulsed in Claire's leg. She yelled in fury and smacked, hit and elbowed him in every possible place. The scab on her arm split and blood trickled.

They rolled in a tangle of pandemonium fueled by primal survival instincts.

Scarecrow landed on top and straddled Claire's waist. His hand swung downward fast. Slap!

The wicked contact jarred her head.

"Not my birthday. Why'd ya say that?" he snarled.

"As..." Claire said, paused and touched the sore spot on her jaw from his most recent hit. She allowed an aura of magical energy to swirl around her head. The bruise grew fast, but her magic dominated with parental love and healed the minor injury completely.

Sweat oozed from scarecrow's pores and formed rivets in the lines on weathered cheeks. When he saw her heal, his eyes flashed with black fury.

Claire twirled fingers in a spiral over her jaw, and then flicked them toward scarecrow's face.

His wickedness didn't stand a chance from the flick of magical parental love. Burns, about the size of quarters, appeared across rough cheeks.

Scarecrow screamed.

"As a warning," she continued in a sing-song voice. "Maybe, I should have said, *happy death day*, instead."

Gnarled fingers grasped her shoulders, squeezed and shook with hatred.

No weapon training? Claire thought as a laugh burst from her in the midst of rough shaking.

She did not know where the emotion and sound came from, it was such a deep reaction, but she knew enough to use it to advantage.

Her laughter incited more daemon rage, but also distracted him.

Claire shifted position, rolled out from under him and got her strong leg under her. Pure bred stubbornness lifted her on the wings of pain and up she went to stand facing him.

"I have a *heart*," she remarked with a smirk.

Scarecrow shoved her backward with wicked,

magical force.

His powerful, vengeful fury sent her flying across the room.

Claire landed hard against the stove, just missing the boiling cauldron. Steam circled around her and clouded her sinuses with the smell of rancid potion.

Instead of harming her, the scented potion brought memory flashing forward from the recesses of her mind.

When scarecrow had used her own shocking power on her, Claire saw the magical electricity journey on nerve endings between her brain and muscles.

Sure, he had stolen her power to shock, but this time she knew exactly how to conquer him. She would project her magical electricity differently.

He advanced while waving the curved blade of his knife.

Wait for it...

Finally, he was close enough.

In a fast move, Claire spun full circle, and then kicked the heel of her blue suede boot at the side of his knee.

On impact, Claire sent the personal memory of him using her shocking power against her.

The magical projection power she realized was a part of her core being during the practice with the bubble assisted now as she sent electrical magic.

She shocked him through the kick by sending the memory of pain into his brainstem, and then encouraged the power to spread to the tiniest nerve endings under his skin.

Scarecrow screamed, collapsed and writhed in

desperate flailing to escape the under skin torment of electrocution.

A throaty growl came from the interior of an old wooden crate in the corner.

Claire ignored the animalistic warning and swept her hand through the air toward the boiling cauldron.

The scarecrow daemon still squirmed on the floor in turmoil.

Claire grabbed empty air as though seizing something invisible. In actuality, she was. With a powerful swing of her arm, she spun and flung the empty air from her palm toward the man.

The boiling cauldron flew through the air on faery glimmer particles and dumped its load on the screaming daemon.

"Extra electricity and wet potion." Claire stood on one foot now because her knee finally quit supporting her weight. "Like I said, happy death day."

Scarecrow's twitching body stilled.

A hound's roar pierced through any sudden sense of accomplishment and survival.

Claire faced the tower of wooden crates.

A large, angry hound leapt from the top of the pile and bounded across the room toward Claire.

She froze, stared directly into the hound's sky blue eyes with anticipation and dread.

The oversized dog pounced, but never landed on Claire.

A feline screech filled the room and Katrina jumped from the crate. During her flight through the air, she transformed from large black cat to human persona.

Katrina landed on the hound's broad back, grabbed long tendrils of fur and yanked as though pulling on reins.

The hound bellowed and transformed into a human.

They scuffled on the floor between the coffin and table, rolling and screeching while magic burst in rays of multicolored potency from their combating bodies.

Claire pressed hot fingers against her forehead and rubbed hard. She forced herself to focus and push yet another shock away.

Katrina came out the victor and wrapped the hound's hands and feet with magical ribbon.

Hot pink satin? Claire shook her head at the absurd contrast to real life conflict bound in ultra feminine pink satin.

At last Claire spoke. "Acala," she breathed, livid with the emotion of betrayal still piercing her heart. "It was you! You told the daemons about my dreams."

"Stupid fae." Acala growled and wiggled in her bindings. "Your magical heritage makes you vulnerable because you can't help but protect and care for the abandoned and homeless creatures of the human world. I slipped in easily."

"Shut up," Katrina commanded. "You know this bitch?" She paused to glance at the scarecrow.

"He's dead," Claire remarked. It surprised her how flat her voice sounded. "Thought I knew her."

A shaking started in Claire's fingertips and traveled up her arms. *It must be shock*, she thought, completely unable to control the trembling. "I electrocuted scarecrow with my zap and the liquid potion. Never knew his name."

"We've got to get out of here," Katrina said, and gagged Acala. "This kennel is marked and the rest of the pack will return—including Grismere. Can you travel?"

"He was a hound?" Claire stared the dead scarecrow sprawled grotesquely on the floor and shook her head. Would she ever fully understand?

Katrina grunted, grabbed the hairy chin and jerked his head around so she could see. "He was a mutt. There are many breeds. Grismere was his sire. This is Radok, Grismere's seventh son."

"But this daemon is old."

"Grismere is much older." Katrina pulled her pink wand from black jeans and snapped it toward Acala. The female hound turned into a small grey stone. "Trust me," Katrina continued, "we need to go." She picked the stone up and tucked it into a round box which she had removed from her jeans.

"Why'd you do that?"

"Grace will want to chat with Acala. Maybe we'll get good info from this despicable bitch. Come on, this is the only way out."

Katrina put the round box into her pocket, led the way to the wooden crate, and began climbing.

"Why not use the door?" Claire asked as she limped across the room. She sucked a quick breath through clenched teeth with every third step.

"Because the door's a fake," Katrina answered. "A trap for you, just in case you managed to get that far."

"Ugh," Claire muttered, pulled herself up onto one of the crates and sat a moment while trying to catch her breath. They needed to get out, but a penetrating exhaustion threatened to overcome her ability to function. A quick touch of the heart locket revived her enough to continue the upward journey.

They arrived at the top of the crates, and Claire realized there was a doggy door installed in the wall. She grunted, got on hands and knees and crawled through. The injured knee collapsed and she went face down in the alley. She groaned, pulled herself a bit further, and tilted against the wall.

A question suddenly popped into Claire's head.

Katrina was busy tracing the doggy opening with her wand.

The high pitched screeching of many voices suddenly filled the alley.

Claire cringed away from hell on wings. That answered part of her question.

Katrina moved to the right of the doorway and allowed the hellion cleaners access to the building.

"It just occurred to me that they didn't appear when scarecrow died. How's that?"

Katrina shrugged. "I didn't know what I'd find inside, so I blocked their access because I didn't want them to get *you*."

"But they clean up evil."

"Not just evil, Claire. They would take you because you're a powerful magical being."

"Humph!"

Katrina laughed, twitched her nose and cat whiskers which appeared as though brought out by humor. "How's your knee?"

Claire picked at the torn jeans fabric and peeked inside. "Swelled. Think I'm too magiced out to fix it."

"Grace can heal you, good as new," Katrina said. "After Leeson has a conniption, that is. You know, I told him I'd bring you back. Let's go." Katrina's hand shot toward her.

Claire experienced Katrina's touch, and then the world blurred into a haze of multi faceted color. Those colors catapulted them through space and time on beams of light.

Magical travel, she thought. *Piffle butt.* Claire closed her eyes to hide the speed of change.

.

| Part Four |
Over the Rainbow
*Hope is that thing with feathers
that perches in the soul...*
Emily Dickson

* * * * * * * * *

[9] Screaming Mojo

Claire and Katrina arrived at their destination on the sound waves of a gentle purr.

"You're purring?"

Katrina laughed. "I love traveling on magical lights and sound waves."

"Ugh," Claire said. "It makes me want to barf. Where are we?" She glanced around at the unfamiliar landscape. Pain pulsed from the injured knee so she grasped the bars of a high privacy gate.

"It's all right," Katrina answered, and moved polished hot pink fingernails across a steel gate lock. "Grace's friend Charles lives here and has offered the use of his mansion for our battle with Weyer."

Katrina walked through the gate and held it open for Claire to follow.

"Fight here?" Claire stepped through with a breath stealing limp and waited while Katrina worked her magic on the closed gate. She paused and focused on getting her breathing in control. Maybe her knee was worse than she had originally thought.

"Yes, we'll fight here," Katrina answered. "We won't let Weyer anywhere near the pyramid because the ground it's built upon is an elemental nexus. I realize you haven't had a chance to study, but that means the Montgomery Block must not fall into wicked possession."

"Montgomery Block?" Claire asked, bent with hands on thighs and squeezing another breath inward.

"The name of the city block as it's known to non-magicals." Katrina watched her with a serious expression. "When we get inside we'll fix your leg."

Claire straightened and took a cautious step. "Usually breathing through the pain helps. Not this time. Take my mind off... You didn't finish. Montgomery Block?" she repeated, and stared at the long driveway while wondering why they couldn't travel into the mansion by some sort of magical means.

"You're a strange one," Katrina said. "The Montgomery Block is the ground where the pyramid was built. Come on," she continued, and pulled Claire's arm over her shoulder. "Let me help you."

They stumbled like a three legged crane toward the mansion.

Claire studied the circular water fountain. She suspected Katrina was responsible for the bright pink flowers floating on the surface. "Grace lives in the top of the pyramid so she can protect the nexus from evil?"

"That's an excellent observation on your part. You're learning fast. The power of the nexus doesn't discern between good or evil. Whoever maintains the land, they can harness the powerful magic for their purposes. Grace uses the magic to help people, both magical and non-magical, but she also protects the city. Weyer would turn San Francisco into an earthside way station for Hades if he had the chance to conquer the land over the nexus of power."

"Hades? Why not just call it hell?"

"Because daemons don't like the disparaging term *hell* used in place of the proper name for their homeland. It's Hades or trouble. I think we have enough trouble raining down on us, don't you?"

"Yes," Claire answered.

"Charles would agree with you. He's an alchemist of great power, and his home cannot be swayed to evil just because a daemon steps within his property lines."

Claire swallowed a lump in her throat. The sound and sensation of water falling gently into the fountain basin relaxed her thoughts slightly. She pulled away from Katrina, sat on the rim and leaned toward the water.

The wetness drew her in.

In slow motion, Claire sent fingers toward the wet surface with mindful intention. A pause, and then in faith, she touched the water and immersed fingertips. A sigh escaped. "I wondered."

"About what?"

"I electrocuted scarecrow," Claire answered. "I've never been afraid of water, but what if the fact he stole my power had changed something and made me vulnerable to anything wet?"

"Oh that's simple," Katrina said, and placed a reassuring hand on Claire's shoulder. "Your power is inborn and belongs to you. He stole your power, but since it wasn't a natural part of him, the theft backfired and eventually killed him."

"Let's go in," Katrina said, and helped Claire stand. "We need to finish preparing for battle and I want Grace to talk to this mutt." She patted her pocket in reminder of Acala's stony presence and led the way through the front door.

Inside, Claire gasped at the beauty surrounding them, but Katrina kept walking.

Trees grew out of the marble floor and an inlaid circle design in the center of the entrance hall was decorated with flowering plants. "Trees inside?"

"Grace did that," Katrina said.

"Claire!" Leeson ran down the stairs and swept her into a tight embrace.

Katrina managed to slip away.

"Are you all right?" he murmured into her hair.

Leeson smelled of fresh air and honey. Claire pressed her face into his solid chest and inhaled deeply. When she exhaled, a groan escaped.

Although she knew absolute safety in his arms, the events of the last day weighed her down with pain and a deep heartfelt longing. "I'm fine—now. But I'm filthy and must look horrible."

"Nonsense," he said firmly, and touched her cheek with a loving caress. "You're alive and beautiful."

"Humph." Claire didn't feel like arguing so she shifted focus. "What have you been doing?"

"We went into the portrait and didn't realize it's a time funnel."

Claire backed away and stumbled against one of the trees. Rough bark supported with an earthly strength. "A portrait? Time funnel?"

"Yes," he answered, and waved toward a landscape painting above one of the double staircases. "Turns out the virtual realm within the gilt frame was penetrated by a water daemon and infused with River Styx water. When we went in it was night, but we came out, it was already day. Even though it seemed like minutes while we were in there, almost twelve hours had passed out here. We had to seal the portrait off from the mansion to prevent invasion from the realm within it during our coming battle."

Leeson fingered the goggles which still hung around her neck. "What's this?"

"A wickedly vulnerable hazard," Claire answered, and pulled them over her head. The strap caught in her hair. "Ugh." She paused and untangled them from hair strands. "We need to put them somewhere safe because whoever wears them can see me in my bubble."

"That's not good," he replied, and took them while studying the magical artifact with interest. "I know the perfect place." He snapped his fingers and the goggles vanished.

"Are you going to tell me where you've hidden them?"

"No," he answered.

"Where's Abraham?" Katrina asked as she came back into the entrance hall from the dining room. "I thought for sure he would still be here."

Leeson eyed her with an air of restraint, rubbed the side of his nose, and then glanced at Claire.

Claire quirked a brow at him and shrugged. She didn't know anything about Abraham.

Katrina had watched Leeson with growing emotions that made her magic morph in ways Claire had not seen before.

Pointed ears moved out of Katrina's head, whiskers appeared and her eyes shifted into feline pupils, narrow slits of black flashed with growing agitation. "Where is Abraham?" she screeched.

"He went with Charles into the portrait to stop the invasion from that point of entry," Leeson answered. "The only way to seal the portrait was to work the spell from that side. Abraham went with Charles so they could combine their elements into one cohesive action."

Katrina roared in fury, spun on her heel and raced up the stairs to the portrait.

"It's sealed. You can't get through," Leeson stated in take charge firmness.

Katrina ignored him and continued toward the portrait.

Grace blended upward from a step. Faery glimmer spiraled around her serene form and she stood firmly in front of the landscape.

Katrina stopped in her tracks. Long cat tail twitching, she said, "I need to help them."

"Abraham will be all right," Grace replied. "He wanted to help stop the water daemon. Calm down, Katrina. We need you here to assist with your created battle warriors. We'll also need all the help we can get for Claire's injury."

Claire moved away from the tree. Dizziness made her head spin. "Oh no," she whispered. "There's something...wrong."

Her injured knee completely gave out. The room tilted. Claire groaned and sent her arms outward.

Leeson caught her before she hit the floor. "What happened?"

Everyone's concerned faces passed across Claire's vision. She didn't black out, but everything spun in a vortex and made the world blurry. She was vaguely aware of being placed on a long table and Grace slicing through her jeans.

"Oh dear," Grace whispered with a prolonged shake of her head. "Since Charles isn't here, we'll need Miles."

A soft wind swept over Claire and Miles arrived

with a fluttering of butterfly wings. "You called, milady?"

Claire struggled to prop herself up on elbows. She stared at the split in her jeans. "Holy Mother!"

Her leg was swelled beyond recognition and mottled black with purple splotches from the knee to her ankle. She groaned and flopped backward.

Pain bruised her mental awareness with a new and growing fear. *What's wrong? How could this happen with a twisted and cut knee?*

"Miles," Grace spoke softly as though she didn't want Claire to hear. "Claire has injured her leg during a skirmish with a filthy hound. I believe she has picked up a flea or parasite. Will you examine her so that we may be sure?"

"Be easy," Miles said, and patted Claire's arm to reassure her. He moved closer to the split jeans and studied Claire's leg.

Leeson squeezed her hand and caressed with feather light touches.

Claire focused on Miles' face although it remained smooth and free of emotion. She figured he kept a straight face because he didn't want her more frightened than she already was.

Finally, she pulled her attention away and faced Leeson. Although he was paler than usual, the strength and loving concern she saw in his expression gave her some relief.

"Miles?" Grace touched Claire's head. "Should we sedate her?"

"No," Miles answered, and straightened. "I'm sorry, Claire. You've picked up a wicked parasite and if we sedate you the herbals will affect the creature so that it can't be removed. It must be fully awake and functional for our extraction to work."

"Ugh." She couldn't vocalize more. She gripped Leeson's hand tight.

"Do you have your pouch of tricks, milady?" Miles asked.

"Of course." Grace tucked a hand into the folds of her blue gown and pulled the same pouch from its depths that she had used for the locket spell. She opened it and spread magically infused instruments on the table next to Claire.

"Then let's begin," Miles said. "Katrina, please stand here." He indicated a spot at Claire's feet, but slightly to the left side. "It's important you don't stand in direct alignment with the bottom of Claire's feet. We must have a free flowing space from head to toes so that she will remain grounded after the extraction."

Miles removed a wand from his sleeve and flicked it toward the floor at the end of the table.

"Why'd ya do that?" Claire slurred as she tried to raise her head. She couldn't see what Miles had done.

"Don't worry, my dear," Miles said gently. "Just a container for the pest we must extract. Leeson, please keep her shoulders flat."

Leeson nodded and laid his forearm across Claire's collarbone.

She tried to smile at him, but her face would not move even for such a simple action.

"You'll be all right," Leeson murmured into her ear, and then kissed with sweet gentleness.

Claire focused on the magical energy of his kiss and wished it would last forever.

Grace and Miles, heads bent over Claire's knee, whispered together in private consultation.

Pain pulsed through her veins. Claire groaned as niggling little sensations spun around under the skin on her knee. She pushed the thought away of little critters crawling around in her magical meridians.

There was a piercing sensation on the bottom of her left foot.

"This incision will be our exit for the creature," Miles said.

Claire cried out. The pain pulsating around her foot was more powerful than any she had ever experienced despite years of physical abuse. She sent her fingers in search of the locket. It warmed her palm, but didn't relieve the newest wave of pain.

"Katrina, you may begin pulling the energy. Use a hand over hand motion as if you are pulling a rope out of Claire's leg."

Claire inhaled sharply and held on to the oxygen as if it were her last breath.

"Breathe, dear," Grace intoned gently.

She stared into sapphire eyes and shook her head.

Grace smiled gently and touched her cheek.

Air moved freely in and out of Claire's lungs. The magical spell took the choice to breathe away.

The motions occurring around her left leg terrified Claire. She didn't understand what was happening.

The pulling down sensation from Katrina's movements reached all the way to the knee and then dragged whatever horrible thing had grown inside her toward the foot.

Claire screamed. She didn't care who heard. Another scream—this time the pitch of sound tore out of her throat with wrenching emotion.

The damn parasite didn't want to give up its new warm home.

Miles swirled his wand.

Grace spoke in a soft voice. Claire thought it was a prayer that she remembered Sister Teresa reciting.

Claire tried to focus on Leeson's face. Shadows colored his cheeks with worry. She squeezed his hand.

He touched her hair with the softness of a lover's caress.

The creature under her skin moved.

Claire flinched upward and screamed in holy terror.

The pain and miniature monster traveled downward toward her foot.

Leeson's arm across her collar bone moved her to lay flat. She closed her eyes. No prayers came to mind. Sister Teresa's face blurred behind closed eye lids. The locket burned in her palm.

She heard whispers, much too low for comprehension from her fog of pain and fear. One hand holding Leeson's, the other wrapped tightly around the locket, she sought the magic of family love to expel the wickedness trying to take over her body.

"Get out!" she screeched, and added another throat tearing scream.

There was an odd *splat* as the thing landed in the container. Miles moved fast, put the lid on the container, and took custody with a triumphant grin.

Claire gasped and lay on the table breathing hard.

"Just a few more minutes," Grace remarked. She began cleaning Claire's leg with a liquid that came from one of the bottles out of the pouch. "Miles, please dispose of that thing properly. I don't want to see it, or another one like it for a long time."

"Yes, of course, milady." Miles used his wand to seal the container and then carried it from the room.

Claire was inclined to agree; she never wanted near one of those nasty parasites again.

The smell from the solution that Grace applied began to relax Claire. She didn't know what it was, but she suspected it had calming properties as well as disinfecting power. She tilted into Leeson's caress upon her hair and let her eyes close in rest.

The energy moving through Claire from head to toe healed in a flowing sensation. She was surprised when the bottom of her foot tickled.

"I've sealed the cut, Claire." Grace spoke with gentle assurance. "It may be tender, but you should be able to walk normally in approximately three days."

"Thank you," Claire murmured as sleep overcame her senses.

[10] Fascination

"Why did you put her to sleep again?" Leeson asked.

"I didn't," Grace replied. "She's exhausted. Don't worry; she won't sleep long—only until we need her."

Grace cleared Claire magically of the other remains of battle; tangled and dirty hair, soot and bruised skin, all became clean with a whispered spell. "She's freshened up now. Let's put her to sleep in one of the bedrooms upstairs. You can carry her."

"All right." He lifted Claire and strode toward the steps. "Hope you're right and she wakes up soon. Do you think we should worry about her dreams?"

"After we tuck her in, I'll put a replica of her bubble around her so that her dreams won't escape."

"I'll stay with her."

Grace quirked a brow. "If you insist."

"I do."

In the bedroom, Grace pulled the coverlet back and waited while he placed Claire gently on the bed. "Wish she hadn't experienced whatever happened." His hand lingered at her fingertips where he thumbed her knuckles, and then slowly pulled away.

"She's strong," Grace replied, "even before we opened the connection with her family. I knew her mother Allyssa. The Rockford family line has powerful magic. Claire has that power within her."

Grace tucked the blanket around Claire. "She won't sleep for long despite her tiredness. There's a seed of knowledge within her and she realizes Weyer will be here soon."

Leeson sat in a chair and watched closely while Grace waved her wand and encased Claire within a bubble. "How will she get out?" he asked, and shifted position in the small chair, trying to get comfortable.

"The magic is set to dissolve when she awakens."

Grace gave him a knowing smile and exited.

Never expected any of this. He suspected Grace had though. She was a great Perceiver of the future, but also always followed the basic tenets of free will. Or so he had always believed.

Fascination, he thought. *The power to hold somebody's attention completely or irresistibly... Enthralled.*

Claire was completely under his skin. Her presence across the room in the sleeping bubble fed a protective urge beyond his usual guardian of the innocent lifestyle.

His fingers tingled and longed to touch her alabaster skin. The sensation extended over his body with the lightness of a fluttering feather. He sighed, leaned back in the chair, and closed his eyes.

Escape into the imaginative fantasy of Claire's love rippled around him dreamlike as he relaxed deeply along the rim of sleep.

She's safe. He stayed there, between sleep and awareness, the gentle sound of her breathing caressing his soul with longing.

"What's happening?"

"Wha?" Leeson jumped from the chair, dagger in hand, and stared around the room.

Claire sat in the bed, eyes crinkled with repressed amusement.

"You all right?" she asked, voice edged with laughter.

"Humph."

"I didn't realize you were sleeping."

"I wasn't," he said, defensively.

"Whatever. Deny it if you want." She patted the blanket over her knees. "I'm much better now. Grace's magic and the power of the locket have completely healed me. And Grace has taken my clothes again."

"Well, there wasn't much left of them," he said while turning slightly away from her and pointing at a door. "The closet is filled. I'll go so you can get dressed." He exited quickly before she could realize that he longed to stay.

* * * * * * * * *

Claire pressed her face into blanket covered knees and muffled laughter. She wasn't sure the heavy ornate door muted sound and her laughter insisted on being expressed.

Leeson's red cheeks and obvious arousal, covered up by quick movements, and defensive posture was pure funniness. It was flattering, too, but laughter won out.

She took a breath, trying to pull the mirth inward. The action just made her shake with heartfelt amusement. Giving up, she laughed aloud, pushed the covers aside and climbed down off the huge bed.

The carpet was soft under her toes. She wiggled them in appreciation, approached the closet, and pulled the double doors open. "Oh my!"

Claire had never dreamed a closet could be so large. The bonus... It was filled wall to wall with clothes and shoes.

"Look at the boots," she whispered in awe and stepped into the walk-in closet. There was no doubt about it, she had a boot fetish. She placed eager fingers on a pair of deep, ruby red over the knee beauties. Did she dare wear something with a heel like that?

The leather hummed under sensitive fingertips.

"Yes," she said with a grin, and lifted them off the shelf.

Next, she went to the slacks and jeans. Although she always wore basic blue jeans because they were best for road travel, two pairs of black leather pants caught her eye.

She decided trying them on was the only way to make the right choice, so she took both pairs of pants off their hangers and placed them aside with the crimson boots.

Lacy undies and a wide variety of tops tempted her next. She frowned at the school girl white blouses and passed them by.

A crimson top caught her eye. The exact same shade as the boots, styled like a camisole and boasting satin lacings, she chose it without a second thought.

She passed a curious item on the way to her growing pile of clothing. It was as if the special piece whispered sweetly in her ear.

Claire paused, pulled the hanger off the closet bar and studied the vest. She had never seen anything like it before. It was made up of pockets, loops and snaps. Attached to one of the snaps were covers that reminded her of elbow length gloves, except these came with the fingers exposed.

The vest was black, looked like it would hug her as a second skin, but was designed with a flounce around the bottom. The look was pure femininity in leather. She removed it from the hanger, picked up her chosen outfit and returned to the bedroom.

The first thing Claire tried on was one pair of the leather pants. In front of the three section mirror, she studied the fit. She tilted her head to the side, gazed at a different angle in the left side mirror, and chewed her bottom lip thoughtfully.

She put the cami on and laced the ribbons. The satin made her wiggle with girly delight. Katrina would probably tease her.

Leeson? Thinking of him made her grin and wonder if he would run from the room again.

Claire decided to try the other pair of pants. When she removed the first pair she discovered pockets in the sides. Maybe that was why they didn't feel quite right?

The second pair slid over her skin like satin. Every inch molded to her curves. They weren't tight. In fact, it was as though her flesh accepted the leather as a long lost part of herself. She sighed with the pleasure of new discovery.

It was such a simple joy, but she suddenly couldn't wait to get the crimson boots on. She sat in the chair previously occupied by Leeson and pulled the left boot on. The zipper glided upward and above her knee with a sweet hum.

Fingers shaking in anticipation, Claire put her foot into the right boot and zipped it up. She sat for a moment and gazed at the place where crimson boot topped black leather pants. Her knee was healed and now covered with double layers of leather for the first time ever.

Claire stood. The heels were higher than anything she had worn before, but her body adapted easily to the extra inches. She strode across the room, picked up the vest and moved to the mirror.

The action of slipping her arms into the vest made her pause and stare at her reflection. She suddenly realized why each piece seemed right in the trying on process. They were meant to be together.

She swallowed a lump in her throat, buttoned the two buttons of the v-neck vest, and then pulled the fingerless gloves on. Smoothing the leather up to her elbows and closing the small zipper on the interior of the arm completed her outfit.

Amazement rippled along her skin. The woman inside the mirror didn't look like an orphan brought up in a convent.

The golden heart locket rested just above her cleavage and black curls sheltered her shoulders.

Black and crimson leather made her alabaster skin glow with a new womanly awareness.

Claire had always worn her hair down, even in the hottest weather. Today, she decided to make a change. Since meeting Grace, she had admired her long silver French braid.

Claire had also never used magic on her hair before. She bent forward at the waist, shook her hair out and fingered through the strands. Then she tossed them back, palm smoothed them and added several embellishments.

She studied the results when crimson ribbon, several soft feathers and earthly crystals interwove through her long French braid.

"Perfect. You're ready for anything, Claire."

In an action of pure playfulness, she spun in a complete circle and stopped facing the mirror again. A grin, and then she left her bedroom ready for anything daemon Weyer could dish out.

Halfway down the stairs, she paused and studied the portrait that Leeson, Grace and Katrina had journeyed into. Hidden in the brushstrokes on the left side, she noticed the wicked face of a daemon watching her. She tilted her head and pointed at him with intent. Then she crooked her finger in a 'come here' gesture.

He blended away.

It was all right. She knew he went to get Weyer.

Claire skipped down the stairs in her three inch heels. After walking through the entrance hall, she discovered Leeson, Grace and Katrina in the dining room.

Leeson stood with his back to her.

"Come in, Claire," Grace invited. "We're having a snack, if you're hungry."

Leeson turned. Surprise registered across his face and the wine glass tilted in his hand. The essence of Annwn's finest grape crop spilled down his shirt front. He fumbled the glass and avoided dropping Charles' sparkling Waterford crystal.

Claire bit back a smile. "Thank you, Grace. Actually, I'm famished." She pulled a chair away from the table and sat. "Thank you for the clothes, too."

Katrina winked at her.

Claire put some roast beef and potatoes on her plate. "I think I have enough time to eat. Weyer's watcher was in the portrait and left when he saw me come downstairs. They'll be here soon."

"You saw a daemon in the portrait?" Katrina asked, and then faced Grace with lines of worry forming across her forehead. "I thought Charles and Abraham fixed the portrait so Weyer couldn't get through. If daemons are watching us, maybe we should worry Charles' plan has failed?"

"Don't worry about Charles and Abraham. I have confidence in their abilities," Grace answered. "The daemons can't penetrate the painting because the canvas has been made rigid. That makes it impossible for anyone to travel through."

"Well, either way, they'll be here soon," Claire said.

"They won't be able to get into the mansion until we let them past the ward." Katrina said. "Nice choice in your battle outfit. I approve."

Leeson choked on his breath.

"Thanks," Claire replied. She winked at Leeson while watching his face get redder.

"Think I need some air," Leeson sputtered and escaped through the opened slider door.

"Don't go far," Grace remarked toward his back. They heard an expletive and the sound of wings.

"You really shouldn't tease him so, my dear." Grace poured Claire a glass of tea. "This will fortify you for the coming battle. You know Leeson still insists that you not be here, but Katrina and I both disagree. Poor man is overwhelmed by three women's stubbornness. I don't believe he's ever encountered such a challenge."

Claire and Katrina laughed.

Katrina pulled the small round box from her pocket. "There's something I wanted to give you, Grace. But I waited for Claire since what I have concerns her."

"What is it," Grace asked.

"This is a hound we captured after Claire killed her attacker." Katrina removed the stone from the box and handed it to Grace. "Claire says she knew her."

"Is that true, Claire?" Grace asked.

"I thought I knew her," Claire answered. "Apparently, she hid her dark side. I didn't realize she was a shapeshifter. She's the reason Grismere knew about my dreams. Acala was a stray that stayed in the back grounds of the convent for awhile. I fed her and built a shelter to keep her dry."

Grace held the small stone in the palm of her left hand. "The proper technique must be used and the left hand serves this purpose because it's closest to the heart."

"You must all know," she intoned in a voice barely above a whisper. "I will not speak to Acala in person. Keeping this enemy interred within an earthly stone protects us."

"How will you know if she is being truthful?" Claire asked. "I've already been deceived by her. I don't want to risk the rest of you."

"As a Perceiver," Grace explained, "I can enter Acala's mind and sift through hidden memories. In this case, her inability to resist my presence within her life history will assist our endeavors."

Grace gave them a reassuring nod, and then closed her eyes while holding Acala's stone form in a relaxed hand. She moved fingers in a gentle waving motion and hummed low.

Claire poked her mashed potatoes nervously and tapped her toes. It was strange that she no longer felt the sting of Acala's betrayal. Instead, there was only the need to discover truth.

Grace must have included emotions when she healed me.

"It's raining." Grace made the observation in an accented voice unlike her usual self. "Acala is injured, hungry and lost..."

Claire dropped her fork and stared at Grace.

Grace spoke in a tone of calmness. "Acala meets a young girl behind Smith's Grocery. It's Claire..." Grace rubbed the stone between her palms. "Several weeks have passed and Claire has healed Acala and given her shelter. They spend hours together wandering the streets and the nearby fields of a local farmer. Claire trusts Acala and confides in her because she thinks the dog cannot tell her secrets."

"Humph!" Claire pushed her chair back, stood and walked to the open slider.

Grace snapped out of her vision. "Just as I thought. Simple fact is, Acala spoke truthfully when she told you she had been sent by her pack. She told Grismere about your dreams. We already knew that." She returned the stone to the small round box. "Katrina, I need you to put this someplace safe."

"No problem. I know a perfect place." Katrina exited the dining room with her usual feline sashay.

"Are you ready for battle, Claire?"

Claire glanced around the room, and then rested her gaze on Grace. "Yes. At first I was scared. But facing that nasty scarecrow daemon, finding out he was a hound, discovering Acala's betrayal and screaming at a virulent parasite in my leg, I feel like Weyer and his legions are just another challenge to overcome."

"You have a refreshing take on everything."

Claire laughed. "I suspect you are responsible for that. Your healing spell must have also taken care of some of my emotional issues. Suddenly, I see everything differently."

"More than likely," Grace stated in her teaching tone, "what actually happened was your fear of the powerful Insight gift that you've had since birth was healed. You should know that once Weyer is vanquished, his legions will not attack further. They are attached to him and go with him when he dies. Frankly, I'm surprised he would insist on being present during our battle. But apparently he wants Leeson and you himself. The thirst for vengeance blinds those seeking it."

Katrina returned to the dining room and was not alone.

Claire paused and stared in curiosity.

Small wispy white and beige creatures with wings light as air hovered around Katrina. One of the creatures said something in a language Claire didn't understand, and then zoomed across the room to study Claire.

"Who are you?" Claire asked the tiny creature.

The sounds that came from its mouth had a sing song tone combined with a bee buzzing hum, and she didn't understand him.

"I've named him Rocky," Katrina said. "This is his partner. Her name is Brigit."

Brigit flew down and fingered Claire's crimson boot. The tiny creature's creamy coloring was veined with a flowery petal pink. The crimson boots seemed to excite her into laughter. Claire chuckled and turned her leg to give little Brigit a better view of the zipper.

After Brigit finished with the boot, she moved up to Claire's forearm. There, she perched and began tugging on the stitching along the zipper.

"No," Claire said. "The stitching holds the zipper in place."

"Brigit has a natural knowing," Katrina said. "I think she's trying to pull your wand out."

"But," Claire said, perplexed by a seed of confusion. "I don't have a wand."

"Sure you do, my dear." Grace approached, took Claire's hand and turned it palm up.

Brigit hovered over the fingerless glove in pixie delight.

"You've chosen wisely," Grace remarked. "This outfit will give you anything you desire in battle. It was created by specialist elves in Annwn. There's a pocket along side the zipper where you have a concealed wand. You have only to pull it out."

Claire skimmed fingertips along the zipper seam and then made a pulling motion away from her arm. A wand materialized and sparkled with the energy and particles of faery glimmer. "Oh! It's beautiful!"

Grace laughed. "The wand has chosen you. Since that's the case, there will be no training necessary." She studied the wand. "Oh yes, it's copper. That's perfect for you because it will magnify your power through its own elemental properties."

"Wait a minute," Claire said. "I thought that having a wand or weapon required special training."

"Normally," Grace replied, "that would be true. Most fae and witches must train for years to achieve master level. As I mentioned, this clothing comes from Annwn. Many do not have the privilege of owning such unique garments. In your case, I thought it was important for your protection and the success of our mission that you would have these."

Claire swallowed a sudden lump in her throat. "Thank you. I hope that I don't disappoint you."

"I don't expect you will." Grace patted her arm with confidence. "There is one very important thing I want to share with you. During this battle many things will be happening all at once. I cannot stress how imperative it is that no matter what happens, you must not be surprised at what you see and experience. Constant vigilance and movement is required."

"What do you mean by surprise?" Claire asked.

"Simple," Katrina said. "Grace is talking about those pivotal moments when you see something unexpected. For example, you hesitated when I brought Rocky and Brigit into the room. If I could see it, an enemy would, too."

"Katrina is correct." Grace waved at Rocky as he zoomed around the table poking at the leftovers. He perched on the rim of a glass and made faces at Claire.

"Understand," Grace continued in teacher mode. "The inaction that can result during the first few seconds of surprise can be deadly. However, if your enemy experiences that moment, then by all means, jump it to your advantage. That's where constant vigilance can save your life."

"All right. I understand."

"Good." Grace gave her a gentle smile and blue eyes misted over. "Remember that while the coming events are important, it's the journey to get here that defines you. Overcoming your recent challenges has connected you fully with your destiny and magic."

"Incoming!" Leeson ran into the room and gave them a warning wave toward the open slider doors.

[11] *Magical Menagerie*

Leeson didn't stop running. He grabbed Claire's hand, spun her around, and then pulled her from the dining room.

Furious that he still insisted she stay out of the battle, she shouted, "What are you doing?"

They rounded a corner and Leeson pressed her against a wall.

One of the marble columns shifted before Claire's eyes. She gasped as an eight foot tall man of marble, resembling Michael Angelo's David, pulled a sling shot over his shoulder and marched battle ready and naked into the dining room.

"We've got to get back in there! Grace, Katrina and...that thing need us!"

Breath coming fast, Leeson leaned in close. "That thing is one of Katrina's toys. She has a penchant for the morphing power of the veins in marble. It'll hold the daemons off for a few minutes."

Claire huffed. "You can't stop me from fighting."

"I know. That's not..." He paused and looked into her eyes. "No matter what happens..." The words caught in his throat. He swallowed and facetted, expressive eyes dropped to her mouth.

Instinctively, Claire's lips parted on a whisper of breath. A tender fluttering of emotions blossomed around her heart. She tilted closer.

A cacophony of battle sounds intruded upon their intimate moment. War cries, smashing furniture and Katrina's feline yowl carried upon the air.

Leeson touched her hair, spun strong fingers around her braid and played with her ribbons.

The intimate caress held her in fascination. "Leeson," she whispered.

He leaned in and kissed her.

The touch of his mouth sent a blush of heat under her skin and she responded in eagerness. She pulled him closer and slipped her arms up and around his neck.

He kissed her as though it would be their last kiss.

She tightened her hold around his masculine strength.

"You can join in anytime!" Grace shouted as she ran by.

Claire and Leeson parted in amorous breathlessness.

Two short roly-poly daemons followed Grace as she headed straight for the circular marking on the entrance hall floor.

Claire started after Grace, but Leeson blocked her with a hand and shook his head. "Grace has this one."

Grace stopped in the center of the circle, gave the monsters a cocky head tilt, shrugged and pirouetted. The blue fabric of her gown spread wide and ruffled the air with scented flowers.

The daemons roared in a wrathful urge to fulfill devilish duty, flashed deadly knives, and charged through the magical lavender planted in the marble circle.

Grace laughed and clapped her hands over top of her head.

"Arrgh!" the first little monster roared.

Pop. Pop.

Both daemons vanished with a groan of despair. Steel blades of dastardly destruction clattered to the floor.

There was nothing left behind of daemon flesh for the hellion cleaners.

The weapons melted into the patterned mosaic. Fresh blossoms bloomed where the knives had been as though a shift of pure goodness came from the wicked weapons.

Grace pirouetted again and exited the magical circle. "The power of flower essences. Gets them every time. You'll miss all the fun if you stay out here." She winked, flipped her wand and reentered the dining room.

Another large David marble man marched past.

At the dining room threshold two daemons with hound heads blocked the marble David. Their bodies were half muscular human and topped with fierce wolf heads. A determined stance made a menacing barrier in the curved archway.

David swung his sling shot, but was too close to the daemons. The marble warrior stepped back, whipped the leather pouch around again and hit the left hound daemon in the eye.

The hound roared in devilish fury and lunged.

Daemon and marble man crashed to the floor and rolled in chaotic pandemonium. Screeching and vicious growls filled the entrance hall with a horrific energy.

Every sound echoed back from the high ceiling.

The second hound daemon noticed Claire and Leeson, bared crooked teeth in a grin of immoral anticipation and jumped over his companion and the marble David.

The approaching daemon hound swung a long hooked tail in whip fashion at them. The tail made snapping sounds, but missed them.

Leeson sprung into action even as he gave Claire a parting look.

Claire nodded, skirted around them, and went to the dining room in search of Grace and Katrina.

The elegant room was a complete disaster as though a tornado had split the room in two. Everything was destroyed. Even two of the trees Grace had planted in the marble floor were splintered down the middle.

The first David lay broken into four pieces, his determined expression of distain looked directly at Claire as though a silent disapproval of her absence.

There was no sign of Grace and Katrina.

Brigit, the pinkish colored eeze, flew in and paused in front of Claire's face. The tiny critter chattered, and then zoomed into entrance hall. When she came back, a whole flock of eezes followed. They swarmed around Claire and led her outside where Claire then heard sounds of combat.

Just as Claire strode around the front western corner of the mansion a mighty daemonic roar deadened the night atmosphere with potent horror.

A lightning flash split the sky. The light and sound pushed waves of air across Claire's cheeks. The sensation gave a painful scratching like a spell gone wrong. She palmed her face and rubbed briskly to get rid of the wicked feelings left behind by the lightning.

Now standing in front of the mansion, Claire saw that Grace and Katrina battled four daemons with wands and water.

Golden light emanated from the circular fountain. The eezes that had joined Claire flew to the closest daemon. He stood seven feet tall and wore leather and steel armor. Protruding spikes over his massive shoulders extended his size even more.

Claire drew her copper wand from the crimson glove, jumped into the fray and attacked a female hound. This one was in her human form, but covered with dog hair head to toe.

The hound growled, and spoke through yellowed fangs. "'Bout time you showed up."

Claire swished the wand and copper fire came out of the end. "Less chat. More action." The flame landed on the hound's breast.

The female daemon screamed and slashed toward Claire's face with a long knife.

Claire stepped back and kicked high. An odd sensation surrounded her as if air molecules held body and soul vertical. Her boot met the lethal blade in midair. Claire grinned, sent a jolt of electricity, and at the same time grabbed water from the fountain.

The wet stream traveling upon faery glimmer splashed across the hound and soaked with deadly accuracy.

The hound pulsated with electric shock, screamed one last time and stilled in death.

Hellion cleaners swooped in and devoured flesh and bones in business like efficiency.

"I need to learn a new trick," Claire remarked, and turned to the next daemon.

She paused in shock.

Katrina jumped in front of her and several things happened at once.

The flock of eeze surrounded a daemon. He was the same one Claire had seen moments before. Large and menacing, he now looked pale and sickly because the tiny winged creatures lifted and carried him toward the fountain.

He realized their plan and began grunting and squirming in frantic desperation. His actions to escape proved completely useless.

The flock of eezes hovered over the fountain, and then released the daemon into the circular basin.

The daemon yowled.

Apparently water and daemon were not a good mixture. Water splashed high and enveloped him in a deadly funnel. Despite the wetness encasing him, he tried running to the edge of the fountain.

Water spouted from his mouth and holes appeared all over his body. Those new holes allowed more water to pour from him. Even his leather armor was broken through and melted away.

The daemon that Katrina had stopped from attacking Claire by gripping him around the neck groaned pathetically and melted along with his partner.

Daemon remains fizzled and smoked on the concrete.

The hellion cleaners screeched, but there was nothing left for them.

"Told you not to pause!" Katrina yelled.

"I know," Claire gasped through fast breathing. Her heart raced under her breast. "Thanks. Never would've thought simple water could do that to a daemon. Where's Grace?"

"It's holy water. Grace went inside. Come on. That's where we'll find Weyer."

They stepped together over the threshold and instantly jumped into the conflict.

Grace battled two daemons by using one of her trees. The branches swung through the air smacking and clawing at the hairy daemons. Grace waved an arm and the tree grabbed the attackers.

Held within the branches, the daemons were raised high in the air and thrown across the entrance hall. Their yells echoed with eerie dread.

One daemon's flight carried him over the stair banister and he hit the ocean side landscape. There was a smacking and cracking sound as though the wall split.

The daemon slid down the painting and crumpled on the stairs. A wet slurping sound filled the entrance hall and the stunned daemon vanished.

Grace's daemon number two had been tossed into the top of another tree. The branches swirled around him like fingers of wood and leaves. The momentum pulled him into the center of the tree where the tree swallowed the intruder whole.

The tree belched.

Claire decided to stay away from Grace's pretty trees. It was at this moment that she realized although her battles were separate from Leeson's, she sensed his every move.

Their mind connection kept them both on high alert for the safety of the other.

You doing all right? she asked Leeson while skirmishing with a squat smash faced daemon.

Absolutely. Watch the little bugger's ears, they're deadly.

Just at that moment, the short daemon wagged his pointy ears. Needle sharp thorns shot from the ear lobes and headed straight for her.

"Thorns? Missed," she said with a smirk, waved the copper wand and tossed the thorns back.

The pointed projectiles pierced his skin. Fire exploded from his interior and he vanished in a puff of green smoke.

"At last! The reward will come to me," said a woman dressed completely in black clothing and concealed beneath a heavy lace hood. She sent a snaking cobra rope through the air toward Claire. The head formed into an opened mouth with fangs ready to pierce the skin.

Claire ducked out of range, spun on her heel and shot copper fire from her wand toward the woman. She missed.

A rough cackle came from beneath the shrouding hood and the witch advanced. The snake slithered around Claire eyeing her as though seeking an opportunity to plunge fangs into her leg.

Claire studied the shrouded figure.

"Mara!" Katrina yelled.

The woman pulled the covering away from her face.

Claire stared at pasty white skin dominated with black eye and lip color.

"I see you've chosen poorly," Katrina said while circling around their opponent.

The snake hissed, coiled and posed in readiness as though waiting for the order from Mara to strike with deadly fierceness.

"And your *goodness* disgusts me, *Katrina*," Mara said, and shot another spell at Claire.

Claire bent at the waist, and then stepped to the side. The left boot heel caught on a broken branch from one of Grace's trees. She started falling. A weird calmness spread over Claire as her body performed in deep instinct.

Instead of falling, a floating sensation came from the same air molecules she had experienced while outside. Claire placed fingertips on her elbows, slid fingers toward her wrists, and then flung hands toward Mara.

Crimson ribbons flew from the fingerless gloves, sped across the air and wrapped Mara in a tight binding.

Claire landed in a soft rolling motion on the floor and immediately rose back to her feet. She pointed her wand at the snake and blasted it with copper fire.

The smell of burnt snake made Claire gag.

"Bitch!" Mara screeched, and struggled against the magical ribbons that bound her wickedness. A bejeweled bone wand clattered the floor.

Claire clenched her fingers and twisted them to indicate tightening.

The crimson bindings squeezed around Mara.

"Now, you'll pay for your betrayal and defection," Katrina said, and shrunk Mara into a small black crystal.

"Defection?" Claire asked.

"She was part of my cat shifter family."

"I'm sorry," Claire said.

"It was a long time ago."

Grismere stood at the front door and emitted a fierce roar. His chest expanded in fury, feet planted on the threshold, he threw a line of black thorns from a crystal topped staff. "You won't take her!"

A whip cracked somewhere.

The thorns that Grismere conjured vanished in midflight.

Claire spun in high alert.

Grace smiled and waved her wand in friendliness.

Leeson rose into the air above them.

"Already done!" Katrina shouted while pointing her wand at Grismere. "Locked in between! Neither inside nor out!"

The threshold, a very potent magical in-between realm, held Grismere frozen within the throes of Katrina's spell.

Grismere's body responded weirdly to the magic. Part of him had tried to shapeshift, but had frozen before he could succeed. Pain seared his expression and he attempted to move locked feet.

Two of Katrina's marble panthers rushed Grismere with fangs and claws exposed. They attacked with twin feline power. The marble cats knocked the hound daemon out of the threshold that kept him locked in place.

Grismere landed on the front portico with a grunt. His magical shift to hound completed in fast motion, but the action was too late. The frozen moments had given the marble panthers a deadly advantage.

The sound of Grismere's neck snapping under strong marble jaws made Claire shudder. She returned focus to Leeson and discovered that Weyer was the last standing daemon.

Leeson, Grace, Katrina and Claire closed in on Weyer, the Marques of Hades.

"I call upon the ancients," Katrina said. "Bring forth the angels four."

Thunder roared and bright white lightning flashed. The mansion shook with earthquake power and four of the marble columns cracked.

Weyer didn't move. It was as if the command of Katrina's spell immobilized the dangerous daemon.

Four angels of exquisite beauty and power came out of the cracked marble columns.

Katrina motioned the angels to surround them.

When the angels positioned themselves, Claire realized they stood at the four points; north, south, east and west.

The last angel stepped into position, Weyer roared and finally moved from the center. He sent a spell of black fire into Grace's flowery circle.

At first the black flames burned with hellish delight. But the more lavender that was consumed by devil's fire, the flowers transmuted the black inferno into a gentle violet flame.

Seeing the violet flames infuriated Weyer. He lunged toward Leeson while brandishing a broadsword.

Leeson transformed his wand into a long blade. They clashed in mortal combat. For every swing of Leeson's blade, Weyer countered the move.

Caught up in the fight, they levitated higher and higher with each pass of their weapons.

"We've got to help!" Claire shouted as Weyer's blade just missed Leeson's head. She shifted position and craned her neck back to get a better view.

"Don't move!" Katrina shouted to be heard above the roaring conflict and magic coming from the combatants. "We must hold position."

Magical black and gold rays cut across the air between Leeson and Weyer. Dueling blades clashed and clanged.

Grace took Claire's hand. "Use your wand and projection power."

A thick black misty shadow entered through the open front doors.

Claire gasped and glanced toward the dining room. Yes, the same thing was happening there. "Grace..."

"Katrina's angels won't let the hell hallow

through. Weyer is trying to desecrate Charles' home. It won't work. Focus on Leeson. You and I are connected through our hands. Use your power."

Claire gritted her teeth. *All right you dirty fiend*, she growled within her head.

He can't hear you, Leeson said through their mind connection.

Good. He won't know then. Claire raised her wand and sent copper flames toward Weyer.

Weyer laughed maniacally and shot a large grouping of black thorns toward Claire, Grace and Katrina.

The thorns zoomed downward.

Claire swept her wand arm wide.

The thorns broke from the grouping and vanished into the oozing black shadow that now surrounded them completely.

Katrina's angels held the imposing darkness of the wicked hell hallow at bay.

"Hurry Claire," Grace whispered, and nodded toward Katrina.

Katrina was pale behind the tattoos that appeared across her forehead and cheeks when she used her magic deeply. Maintaining the marble angels was draining her power.

Claire yelled in fury, clasped her wand tightly and blasted Weyer with everything she had. Her magic hit the daemon at the same time Leeson's blade swung.

The combined supernatural hit sent Weyer crashing to the floor. Downward he fell, arms and legs flailing and desperate roaring coming from his mouth.

At the end of his three story drop, he landed in Grace's magic circle.

It only took a moment, brief as a blink of the eye and the violet flames burned him away into nothingness.

With its master dead, the hell hallow receded, and then exited the mansion.

Katrina sank to her knees with a strong outward breath. Her angels moved back to their columns and blended seamlessly into the marble. There was no sign left behind that they had ever existed.

Leeson descended slowly, landed next to Claire and folded her into his arms. He kissed the top of her head while repeatedly murmuring, "Thank god."

Grace conjured a couch for Katrina and guided her to its soft cushions. "You take a break. You've earned it. I'll start the cleanup or Charles will never let me visit again."

Claire laughed into Leeson's chest and tilted back. "We'll help as long as you take care of those hungry trees."

[12] Òran Mór

Now resettled back at the pyramid, Claire opened an exterior door in her bedroom. She stepped through and walked to the edge of the observation deck. The railing was high enough to protect from falling yet low enough to allow viewing.

Seeing San Fransciso from the air took her breath away.

The landscape spread outward and included an awesome view of the Pacific Ocean. The bay bridge dominated the area with it's brilliant orange-red color of distinctive refinement.

Although Claire's knees shook from a lifelong leeriness of heights, she still loved the panoramic view.

Overhead, the end of a rain storm had left clouds shaded with hues of grey, light blue and gentle white. The sun blossomed through their wispiness and streaked a golden glow across San Franscisco Bay.

Claire took a deep breath and released it slowly. The sensation gave her closure to the day. So much had happened in such a short period of time. Sunset enjoyed from this high point of view gave hope a new meaning and beginning.

Hope. For the first time in months she experienced an uplifting in her spirit. Her future wouldn't always be so uncertain.

The call of a falcon carried on the breeze. Claire shielded eyes from the sun's low hung orb and searched the sky.

The bird called again, circled and gradually decended to the observation deck.

A flutter around her heart told Claire all she

needed to know.

Leeson, in his animal form, landed and eyed her with a keen gaze.

"You gave me hints," she whispered, unsure whether she should step closer. "Air is my friend, you said."

He ruffled his feathers and walked along the barrier until he perched close.

Even knowing his idenity, Claire moved slowly. At last, she touched silky feathers.

He leaned into her caress.

"Hunter, protector, and warrior," Claire said as she stroked. "I admit, I never expected magic to open this door. Will you transform?"

He pressed his head into her palm for a brief moment, and then took flight.

The suddenness of spreading wings made her gasp and step back while she stared at Leeson.

In midair he transformed. He floated down and landed with silent gracefulness. Last to change, strong wings spread wide, folded in, and then blended into his back.

Leeson appeared in human form wearing a white tee shirt, denim jeans and his long coat. "You're nervous."

"No," she answered. "It makes perfect sense. Even in the cemetary the mask you removed was a bird. I thought you wore it to cover your identity."

"I did," he said. "Battling the hounds was easier in my human form. Since they don't know about my falcon identity, they wouldn't make the connection."

"So it's a secret?"

"Only a few know."

"Is that why you didn't say anything to me?"

He moved closer. "No. If you think about our

situation, there really wasn't time. There was constant danger from the moment we met. My main focus was to get you to safety."

His nearness made her yearn for even more closeness. She faced the ocean view and studied the effect of sunrays across the bridge.

Leeson stepped behind her. "Claire."

Her name carried on a whisper and teased her deepest longing. She tilted back into him. "It's true. There wasn't time. Every moment was filled with fleeing and..."

She experienced a block of hesitation.

"It's okay." He spoke low and his accent grew stronger in husky arousal. "I feel the same."

She shut her eyes. That action focused her other senses on Leeson's closeness.

Everything. He was the universe.

Their shared proximity blended her aura with his.

Claire experienced Leeson on such a deep level that his heartbeat breathed around hers.

"I've always denied the possibility of finding love," she whispered.

Leeson wrapped his arms around her waist and held her gently. "I understand. Our connection is different than your previous experiences."

She faced him. "You won't hold my past against me, will you?"

"Never." His warm breath caressed her face with longing.

"Tell me," she breathed. "What do you feel?"

He kissed the tip of her nose, and then rested his forehead against hers. "Your heart, and I'm pretty sure it's your spirit I feel hugging me."

Claire's arms were not around him. Her fingers paused in caressing his chest. She quirked a brow.

"Hugging?"

"Don't move." Leeson stood perfectly still. "Focus on your heart."

Claire allowed the aura of his magic to blend with hers. The essence magnified and embraced them like the feel of soft rose petals.

An airy sensation became a pulsating expression of craving.

Leeson's lips so close to hers invited exploration.

Still, she didn't move.

The world around them slipped away from Claire's consciousness.

Finally, Claire experienced what Leeson wanted her to understand.

She was one with the universe.

So was Leeson.

Their intimacy and magic entwined on levels she had never dreamed possible.

A deep sigh escaped. As though she had waited an eternity, she pressed against his lips.

The simple joining sent her flying.

There was no fear—only pure joy.

Claire wrapped her arms around him and allowed the magic of his kisses to carry her away.

Leeson's sensual laugh played along her skin. "Did you see the rainbow?"

"No," she answered and nibbled his neck.

He backed away. His sudden absence startled her to their surroundings.

High above San Franscisco, he spun her in a waltzing circle.

Claire gasped. "Can people see us?"

"Only if you want them to."

Arching over the bay and iconic bridge was the largest rainbow she had ever seen. "Oh! The colors are awesome! Do you think it's a sign that everything will work out?"

He moved curls from her neck, kissed and finished with a breath across wet skin. "Rainbows are a symbol of hope."

She had just been thinking of hope, moments before Leeson arrived. "It's perfect. Hope is heart magic. I never really made the connection before though. Emily Dickinson said, 'Hope is that thing with feathers that perches in the soul and sings the tune without the words and never stops...at all.'"

"Then I agree with Emily Dickinson. Can you hear the music?" he asked.

"From a rainbow?"

"Let the earth whisper," Leeson said while spinning. "The ancient Celts called the phenomen Òran Mór. That is the name for the earth's song and is magic at the deepest level."

Claire focused on opening to hearing any possible sound. At first she only heard city traffic, but then something else murmured past her ears.

The heartstrings of heaven and earth combined into whispers of beautiful music. It was powerful and exhilarating.

Leeson's arms surrounded her.

The air around them colored the sky with brilliance scented in delicious aromas of cinnamon and strawberry.

Fear of flying did not exist anymore as they journeyed through the wispy rainbow colors.

Nature's gift of misty transparency caressed them with divine love. Each rainbow color contained its own flavor, sound and intense vibration.

When Leeson guided her flight into the brilliant orange mist, Claire's mouth watered at the luscious citrus scent. Oranges and lemons were already her favorites. She would never see them the same way again.

By the time they reached the enriched shades of violet, joy consumed her and she spun in happy circles while coursing invisible across the San Francisco Bay heavens.

There was no timeline in their current momentum.

Sunset in the western sky gleamed with breathtaking brilliance, and kissed the edge of the earth goodnight.

Claire and Leeson paused in midair above the tip of the San Francisco pyramid. Leeson swept Claire into his arms and kissed with a searing passion.

In slow motion, they floated down to the observation deck.

Claire laced her fingers with Leeson's and guided him into her bedroom.

"Claire," he murmured against the skin beneath her ear. "Are you sure?"

She paused, studied his features, and then went up on tiptoes. "Absolutely." She kissed him and moved their locked bodies toward the bed.

Their laughter comingled as they stumbled while kissing and fumbling with clothing.

Leeson drew back and buried his hands in her hair. "I watch your every move. You're beautiful. The way your hips sway, your hair moves as if on the magic of faery glimmer and the way your eyes crinkle when you laugh. Never stop, please."

"When I first met you, in the park and then the cemetary, I thought I didn't like you." Claire sat on the edge of the bed and removed her left shoe.

"I could tell," Leeson remarked with a laugh. He

knelt on one knee and took her right foot into his hand.

Claire watched in fascination as strong fingers massaged her ankle, and then removed her shoe. "I think it was my Insight gift confused by the roller coaster ride of so many changes happening at once. Everything seemed so unpredictable for a bit."

Leeson set the shoe aside and continued her foot massage. "But just because you didn't like me—that didn't change the fact that I was there to help you. Sometimes the most pivotal moments in our lives happen on a fast track."

Strong hands moved up her leg.

Receptive to his touch, she allowed the fascination of arousal to sweep her into absolute bliss. "Yes," she moaned, "pivotal indeed."

When Claire wrapped her legs around Leeson, he lifted her and lay her back on a soft bed of rose petals. The scented silkiness brushed her skin with the promise of sensual pleasure.

Clothing vanished magically, but in a slow strip tease as Leeson murmured against her skin with gentle butterfly kisses.

They laughed low, but continued with the arousing play.

Claire accepted his loving nibbles and encouraged more with heated touching. Low sounds of ecstasy became the favorite music of the moment.

She flowed in a natural rhythm to their dance of love.

Leeson's tongue teased with strokes of growing passion. His hands, stong yet gentle, found places on her body that had never experienced such pleasure before.

The newness of precious sensations melted her center and a cry of pleasure burst from within as she pressed against him. Trembles under her skin intensified and Claire gave in to the deep yearning for release and arched upward.

With her body momentum increasing, the rose petals lifted from the sheets on faery glimmer. She smiled, pulled Leeson to her mouth and kissed him with wanton urgency. Then she nibbled his ear and encouraged him to enter his longed for home. "Can't wait another second."

Leeson kissed her again.

Claire responded, and then guided his entrance.

Hearts thrumming in tandum, they surrendered to the dance of life with joyous abandonment.

Claire screamed in orgasmic release.

Leeson breathed across her breasts and buried his face in her hair at the base of her neck. "You are amazing."

She wrapped arms around him and caressed down his back where she could feel scratches. "You make it so," she murmured.

He rolled onto his back and took her with him.

They lay in restful bliss, gently touching in sensual appreciation.

"I can still hear it," Claire whispered against Leeson's chest.

"Hear what?"

"Òran Mór. Its purity is also a melody in harmony with your heart beat."

Leeson kissed her on the top of the head, wrapped her securely in his arm, and drifted into slumber.

Claire rose up slightly and studied his

expression of total relaxation. She touched his temple. "You've given me my life back. Thank you. This has to be true love. If it isn't, I don't know what is. Besides, who else could use a rainbow as foreplay?"

The corner of his mouth tucked upward slightly. In sleep, he guided her head to his chest.

Claire snuggled and listened to the rhythmic pulse of his heart until her own pleasant dreams came upon blissful faery glimmer.

Epilogue

Grace, the Colclough of Annwn, loosened the soft draping fabric which rested upon her head in hood like fashion and released it down to her shoulders.

The cloth weight mantled her with the responsibility faced by her position of power. She stood next to the viewer and gazed into the misty center.

"It is done," she remarked. "Will you return to Annwn now, or go south to Florida?"

Black Bryan, Fae Royal Highness, Worthy House of Triton, stepped from the shadows. "Nay," he said with a pronounced highlander brogue.

He nodded at the sleeping couple surrounded by the intimate magical residue from their passionate lovemaking.

"Grace," he said. "I have always known ye to be a temptress. But a manipulator of such magnitude? Ye stun me, even at my age."

She laughed. "Good to see I can still turn your head."

"Mumph," he replied, although the hint of a smile passed over handsome features. "'Tis a necessary deed for sure, but must ye relish it so?"

"I have no regrets, Bry. Don't you see? Claire has been alone since my dear sister passed. Soon that empty place in her heart will be filled with another's love."

Grace paused and brushed fingertips across the viewer controls. "No, I will never regret bringing Claire and Leeson together. Soon she will have her angel and we will have the promise of a hopeful future."

"Will you tell Leeson?"

"He's smart," she answered. "He'll figure it out on his own. He already knows who Claire is. My question is, what are *you* going to do about Florida?"

He shrugged broad shoulders. "That's another story. I best be off. Good evening to ye."

"Be well, old friend," she said softly. "Give my love to Morna. I miss my oldest friend of the heart so much."

"Aye. Will do. Ye must visit her soon." He swung his plaid around broad shoulders and vanished into the colorful depths. Only the earthy scent of highland heather remained where he had been.

Now, Grace stood alone. She touched the surface of the viewer and watched as the sleeping lovers blended away. "Yes, dearest Claire. Your angel will arrive soon."

Magic Never Ends

ABOUT AITHNE JARRETTA
WWW.AITHNEJARRETTA.COM

Once upon a time Aithne Jarretta tripped upon a ley line. Actually it had happened before, but she didn't realize the ramifications until later. She brushed the incident aside and climbed into her car.

Real life was the important factor at the moment. However, those RL moments wove into meeting new friends—the kind most people never see and definitely don't chat much about. Those friends came with persistent voices.

Eventually Aithne brought them out of the closet and politely called them Muses. They became her virtual traveling companions and still journey with her today.

Author: *Claire: the Lost Fae, Concentric Circles, Wyndy: In a Heartbeat, and Kissing Santa.*

www.ingramcontent.com/pod-product-compliance
Lightning Source LLC
Chambersburg PA
CBHW070923130626
46555CB00001B/258